I dedicate this book to my wife Janice,
for putting up with many silent evenings
as I sat in my own little world writing.

You are my rock, you complete me.
Thank you.

Shiralyn J. Lee

Shiralyn J. Lee

LOVING THE PINK KISS

GOLDEN SKY

Golden Sky
New York

Golden Sky is an imprint of *Mondial*.

Shiralyn J. Lee: Loving The Pink Kiss

© 2011 Shiralyn J. Lee

This book or parts thereof may not be reproduced in any form, stored in a retrieval system, or transmitted in any form by any means — electronic, mechanical, photocopy, recording, or otherwise — without the prior written permission of the publisher or the author, except as provided by United States of America copyright law.

ISBN: 9781595692252
Library of Congress Control Number: 2011938239

www.goldenskybooks.com

Introduction

Sarah Niles is 32 years old and the kind of girl who loves to party; shag Jake; a guy that she sees on the odd occasion and slip into a deep drunken sleep every Friday night. Her lifestyle although not boring, had become typically routine and Sarah was beginning to feel as though she needed some excitement to keep herself from going insane.

Jessica; her best friend had been informed by a work colleague Debs; that she had a friend in desperate need to stay in the country. This friend Robbie; a Canadian has amazing blue eyes and a really nice smile apparently. Robbie has a limited time to stay in the country before being asked to leave, courtesy of her majesties service. So a plan (more like a scam) was set in place that marriage would be the answer to ensure a guaranteed postponement to Robbie's current situation.

This is where Sarah stepped in; not just to look like the big martyr because the five thousand pounds payment that was offered took precedence over that, but for the simple fact that she simply just could. But please bear in mind that she was completely pissed when she so politely put herself on offer to be the dutiful wife and missed the fact Robbie is actually a woman.

Sarah didn't have to lift a finger; Debs took complete control of everything. She arranged the registry office and the date and all Sarah had to do was show up on the big day. She hadn't even met Debs in person yet as all arrangement details had been passed on via Jessica. But Sarah didn't care about minor details because if she had listened a little more carefully she would be clued in to the incredible journey that she was just about to embark on.

This story begins on the morning of the wedding and Sarah is preparing herself diligently, it seems that she pays so much more attention to her vanity than she does to her circumstances.

CHAPTER ONE

FOR THE LOVE OF IMMIGRATION

I am doing the right thing, I know it. I thought to myself, staring into the mirror.

"Its 11.15 are you ready yet?" Jessica shouted trying to make me hurry even faster.

"Yes I'm just about done." I replied rather snappishly. That was about the zillionth time she had called me, anyone would think that it was her getting married today. "But these heels are a fucking nightmare. I hate wearing new shoes for the first time!" Now where did I put those god damn plasters?

"Ok Sarah the cabs here, I've got your bag so let's go." Now she's my mother.

"Fine I'm coming let me just grab this." I picked up a cold piece of toast with strawberry jam on it and stuffed it in my mouth whilst we ran down the steps to exit the building.

"Where can I take you to my lovelies?" The cab driver asked in a jolly manner.

"Hi we're going to the registry office on Bow Road could you get us there as fast as you can please we're a little on the late side." Jessica sweetly asked putting on her poshest expression.

"Why certainly maam, I'll have ya there in a jiffy." He replied with a singing tone to his voice.

"Watch out you almost hit that cyclist." Jessica scorned him and then mouthed the word sorry to the cyclist through the window as we drove past.

"That's ok; I've had plenty of practice dodging those slight beggars." He chuckled.

"Oh for God sake I just spilt jam on my top. Jessica I look like shit now, what am I going to do? That's it I can't go ahead with this anymore. This is a sign for me not to go through with it. I've realised it's a stupid idea and I want to go home before I make a big fool out of myself." My nerves had set in and I began to wonder what kind of an idiot I was for agreeing to go through with this scam in the first place. Yes the five thousand pounds I'd received certainly helped sway me and perhaps if I gave it back I could still get out of this but there had been no logic or sound reasoning for my decision in this outrageous matter.

"Look you don't have to get hysterical." She snapped. "First of all you're not marrying this guy to live with him. All you have to do is say I do and then fuck off. Here I have a femme fresh wipe you can use to clean that splodge. Now do you still want to do this or would you rather go home because I'm here for you hun? And maybe I can tell Robbie that you just couldn't go through with it, after all it's not like we know him and have anything to feel guilty about." She pulled out her lippy and perfectly plastered another layer on without using a mirror. I'd always admired her for having that talent.

"No! No I'll do it. I've already said I would and I don't want to disappoint anyone." This was one of those things that I totally regretted agreeing to but I knew that I had an obligation to go ahead with; something other than the money was driving me tho, like a force of nature. I knew deep down that I would have done this regardless whether a payment had been made or not.

"Ere we are then ladies, I got you here safe and sound, Bromley public hall. That'll be eleven quid even." He smiled politely and held his hand out waiting for one of us to pay up. Maybe he should have knocked a fiver off for turning up so bloody late.

"There you go keep the change. Now Sarah are you sure you still want to go through with this?" She was giving me my last chance to escape doing the dreaded deed and I toyed with the idea just for a second but nothing was telling me to not do it.

"Yep ready as I'll ever be!" Neither one of us had thought this through properly and had paid little attention to any consequences that may occur.

"Ok then, let's do it. Look there's a crowd of people waiting and there's Debbie waving like a frantic idiot. Hi Debbie this is Sarah, Sarah this is Debbie, so which one is Robbie?" Jessica questioned her then gripped my arm as we raced up the steps.

"Just get inside they've called for you twice." She replied and herded us inside the hall like cattle on a ranch. "Quickly come on now let's hurry people are waiting"

As we were ushered into a small room I looked around for the person I was about to be wed to wondering why he hadn't had the balls to approach me and at least say thanks for saving his grateful Canadian ass. Jessica sat in the front row and I stood in front of a long table with a black marble top and gold painted legs. Two women were standing on the other side of it. One was wearing the most awful beige suit and the other in a sage green jacket and black trousers and obviously thinking she looked fantastic in that God awful red lipstick that she's probably had since 1970. And that hair, it looked like she had gone for a rewiring job on her last visit to the salon.

Behind Jessica four seats were filled with women that I couldn't identify. They must be Robbie's relatives I thought. Standing next to me was a slim but fit built woman with short dark hair, blue eyes, and pretty cute looking. She was wearing a white suit with a white carnation pinned to the lapel. "Who are you? And which one is Robbie?" I whispered to her and why was she standing at my side?

Before she could answer the registrar introduced herself and her colleague and announced that we were all in the presence of Sarah Niles and Robin Page on this joyful occasion.

I must have missed something. Robbie wasn't here yet. I swung round to look at Jessica for confirmation on what was happening but all I could see was her mouthing; "Sarah I'm sorry! I had no fucking idea."

I didn't understand why she was saying that until I saw the group of women seated behind her smiling happily and patting their weepy ridden eyes with tissues and looking directly at the woman standing right next to me. The sudden realisation that Robbie was actually present hit me pretty damn fast. I was marrying the woman standing next to me, the same sex as me; I was entering into a same sex marriage!

What the fuck? I thought to myself, what do I do now? How the hell do I get out of this one? But I had made a promise to help this person, oh God what have I gone and done? I could feel the sweat beading down my forehead and my stomach was starting to turn over with a feeling of sickness creating a dizzy sensation. There was one thing that had failed to have been mentioned in all of this, that one tiny little detail, one little word. Robbie was a woman. She had never been referred to in the he or she context. Or if she had, that I had been so oblivious to the possibility that someone would assume I would just do it anyway. All I could remember being said was dark hair, good looking, nice smile and kind of shy. My heart was beating fast and my chest began to tighten as my adrenalin kicked in so I excused myself from the room and heard a gasp come from one of the tearful ladies as I legged it out into the hallway. Jessica swiftly followed me and instead of the expected serious questioning and what the fuck comments we just looked at each other and burst out into a fit of hysterical laughter. Could this really be happening to me? Three weeks ago I offered to help out Jessica's work colleague; the wonderful Debs, who just happened to mention that a friend of hers needed to stay in the country and that marriage, was the quickest way to secure it. I peered in through the slim piece of glass at the side of the door and caught a quick glimpse of Robbie smiling at me and made a mental note that she does have a nice smile. Whoa what was I thinking? I don't admire feminine features on another woman. I have to say no! I can't do this! Oh but I agreed to do it, how can I go back on my word now. This person's situation depends solely on my decision and why had no one else come to her rescue; did she not have any friends that could have committed themselves to this illegal scam? This was the perfect time to walk out and never look back but I was already back on route to my bride to be and as I approached her I made my apologies for making such a quick exit and then announced to everyone that I was now ready to continue.

The registrar began to speak but all I could hear was blah blah blah. It was like living in an episode of a cartoon when the grown-ups talk was muffled. Oh how I wanted to not be a grown up right at this moment. Then I heard it; "Repeat after me; I Sarah Niles take thee Robin Page in.........."

I could feel my mouth moving and sound was coming out but I had no idea what I was saying. Shock had started to play a role in this cruel joke. Then I felt my hand being lifted lightly into the air and a gold band was being placed on my finger. Her skin was soft and silky to the touch and her smell was irresistibly fascinating. Then there was a polite applause and voices congratulating us from the crowd on our marital union.

When I finally snapped out of my daze I found myself sitting in a pub with my fourth drink of champagne in my hand and a rather large woman with her arms wrapped around me and kissing my cheek. Jessica was sitting opposite me with her head in her hands sobbing uncontrollably and saying that she was so sorry for getting me into this shit. I quickly downed my drink and pledged for another and then another straight after that. Robbie sat silent just sipping her beer but I did notice that her eyes were focused on me the entire time. Then this large woman who ever the hell she was handed me an envelope with a card inside. There were several signatures written in it with little quotes of good wishes for our marital success and a rather attractive looking confirmation letter showing a room booked for one night at a hotel. This was a rather extravagant hotel that sat nicely next to Tower Bridge and overlooked the river.

A cab driver came into the pub and shouted cab for Niles Page! My bride and I were then shoved into the cab and waved off by everyone and I could see Jessica waving remorsefully with tears flowing down her face. The journey to the hotel was short but awkward and silent and I could feel Robbie's eyes staring at me as I looked out of the window the entire way. All I could think was what the fuck had I just done? Her silence wasn't doing her any favours with me either; could she not just thank me for putting my life on hold in her honour

Chapter One: For the Love of Immigration

or was she just considering whether she had made a good investment with her five thousand pounds.

Once inside the hotel the receptionist greeted us with a nice welcome and informed us that our king size suite was ready. I explained profusely that that was out of the question and that we required single beds in our room. She searched her computer screen for a few minutes only to inform us that everything else was taken. There was no choice we had to accept the suite, and a rather old looking gentleman claiming to be a porter showed us to our room which was on the fourth floor and was situated overlooking the bridge and the river. The ride in the lift was intense; a couple who were on their honeymoon were all over each other and making sloppy kissing noises. It was annoying and rude in my opinion. It would have been much easier to have gone our separate ways and buggered off home to..... home to what; four walls and a fucking T.V? Maybe in my desperation and loneliness I had been drawn into this scam just to gain a little excitement in my life.

Once inside the suite we were confronted by a large bed with cream sheets and a burgundy throw and rather large plump pillows. It practically filled the room. There was also a large couch by the window just big enough to sleep on.

My first words to my new wife were; "one of us can sleep on that I suppose."

Speaking in her soft Canadian accent she quickly offered to do the honour. But I suggested we flip a coin for it, guess what, I should have taken her up on her offer and shut my big fat gob. Sleeping on couches definitely wasn't my forte.

I sat on the big plump cushions and looked over at the dynamic bed I had just lucked out on. It kind of ended my day on the same note that it had started with.

"I'm eternally grateful for what you have done for me." Spoke this quiet soft voice. "I promise I won't intrude on your life and that I'll stay out of your way and I definitely won't bring any one back to the house."

"What house?" I asked in surprise to her comment.

"Yours, you did agree that I could stay with you, didn't you?" She had a slight confused look about her as if I should know what she was talking about.

"The only thing that I flaming well agreed to was to sign a piece of paper and that was all. There has been no offering of sharing my home with you, I think that there has certainly been a miscommunication on your side, I was led to believe that I would never have to see you again." I was furious at the assumption of this woman and I was going to call Jessica first thing in the morning to sort this whole mess out.

I had no idea that she was expecting to live with me. None of this had been decided in any of the conversations I'd held with Jessica. I had assumed that I would be signing divorce papers in the near future and posting them off somewhere. Alarm bells were starting to ring loud in my head but exhaustion from the events of the day and all of that Champagne I had drunk had taken its toll on me for the evening. I lifted my legs up onto the couch and laid my head down and immediately fell asleep.

I awoke the next morning to find a throw had been placed over me and breakfast consisting of croissants and bacon, sausages and scrambled eggs sat on the table. It smelt so good. Robbie was sitting on the edge of the bed with her legs crossed and her head supported with her hands clasped together underneath her chin. She had been watching me sleep, probably for a while as she looked quite refreshed and ready to go. Good morning was passed between us and then I remembered she wants to come home with me. Oh god I'm fucked. My hair was full of static from the velvet fabric probably because I had tossed and turned all night from such an uncomfortable sleep.

"Look, I know that I agreed to marry you to help keep you in the country for whatever reason you may have to stay here but living with me wasn't on the agenda. Do you not have anywhere else to go?" I was pushing for her to come up with an alternative residence so that I could be free of her baggage and carry on living the life that I was accustomed to.

Chapter One: For the Love of Immigration

"Maybe a friend of mine can take me in although she's not exactly thrilled with me going through with this idea. I'm sorry to have assumed that you would do more than you already have and I apologise for the inconvenience that I must have caused you." She had a disappointed look on her face and I could see that she felt very humble towards me.

"No wait a minute!" I yelled out having a sudden change of heart. "Maybe you can stay at mine for a short while, just until we can figure this mess out. But this will only be a temporary option, ok." I had realised that she was in just as much of a mess as I was and that it was my naivety that had led us to this point.

She nodded in agreement and picked up one of the plates and offered it to me and I opted for the sausages and eggs and probably ate like a pig as I was totally starving. It was at this moment that I looked directly into her eyes for the first time and was drawn in by their intense colour.

"You have azure blue." My thoughts were spoken out aloud without them meaning to be.

"Pardon me, you said something." She patiently waited for my reply knowing that I had spoken without thinking first.

I looked away quickly and changed the subject. "Oh it was nothing. I was just wondering where about in Canada you are from. Your accent is very soft and subtle." She gave a slight smile and informed me that she was from Vancouver and that her reason for needing to stay in England was one of dire emergency.

"I will fill out all of the necessary paperwork for immigration services and all you have to do is sign them, if that's ok with you Sarah?" She said my name with such grace that it gave me a feeling of warmth. It felt natural to hear my name flow out from her lips.

"Yes that's fine; whatever, any how I suggest we better make our way back to my place soon, but first I really must eat some more of this delicious breakfast." I scoffed the remains of my food down then put the rest of my wedding attire back on. Hopefully Robbie couldn't smell the vagina cleanser that I had used to clean it.

Upon arriving back at my place I noticed how much of a pigsty I lived in. My clothes were strewn all over the lounge floor and two half cups of cold coffee joined by a half eaten piece of toast had been left on the kitchen counter; it wasn't my usual choice in breakfast normally coffee would suffice.

"Oh God you must think I'm a real pig." I pointed out as I cringed in shame. "I just like to live in a chaotic mess. So you'll find your room just down the hall on the left. You can park your stuff in there and please feel free to make yourself at home. I'm just gonna pick this crap up off the floor and make it a little more presentable in here." House proud I wasn't, and my mother had always cleaned my room and fussed after me when I was growing up so I never had the urge to do much of it.

"Oh please let me help, it's the least I can do and I'm pretty good with a vacuum." She began picking up my state of disorder and stacked it into a neat pile on the sofa.

"Well ok then, I've never been that great at housework myself so feel free to knock yourself out. Do you mind if I go and have a shower, I really need to get out of these clothes?" I was the kind of girl that put my own personal appearance before housework and I think it showed.

For a short moment there was a sense of unfamiliar awkwardness between us as we passed each other in the hallway. To save any further embarrassment I darted into the bathroom where I could regain my composure. I must have been in the shower for more than half an hour when Robbie knocked on the door.

"Sarah your friend is on the phone, do you want me to tell her you'll call her back shortly?"

"Oh no that's ok I'll just be a minute. Tell her to hang on a sec for me will you." I rinsed the shampoo out of my hair as quickly as I could and as I stepped out of the shower I realised that I had forgotten to pick up a towel from the closet in my bedroom. And my bathrobe was on my bedroom floor where I had discarded it the day before. My filthy clothes lay in a crumpled heap on the floor and it

Chapter One: For the Love of Immigration

would have defeated the purpose of cleansing the days grime from my body if I were to put them back on. This was becoming a bit of a dilemma for me and my options were to call to Robbie for help or to make a mad dash for it to my room. I chose the latter and opened the door slowly.

She was nowhere in sight, so I slowly crept along the hallway making sure not to make any noise. Droplets of water were forming tiny pools on the wooden floor and I was being cautious not to slip over on my ass. Finally I made it to my room and I quickly closed the door behind me. As I walked towards the closet I noticed a slight difference on my carpet. I could actually see it. Robbie had been an ideal house guest already and tidied up all of my crap. I was actually starting to feel glad that I had made the decision that she could stay, when I noticed a movement from behind the closet door. Then without warning she appeared right in front of me. There I was, dripping wet, totally naked and full on embarrassed. I was horrified and scanned the room for any remnant that I could use to cover my body. She'd fucking tidied everything up and my hands were working overtime trying not to reveal any more of my assets.

"I need a towel!" I squealed still searching for anything to cover my body with.

"Sarah I'm so sorry, here please take this from me." She reached into the closet and handed me a large bath towel whilst keeping her eyes shut tight. "I'll leave you to get dressed then, I'm sorry for upsetting you and don't forget that your friend is still waiting on the phone." As she left the room I jumped onto my bed and picked up the phone.

Jessica was screaming into the mouth piece, "What's going on and are you alright Sarah, should I call the police?"

"Hi Jessica it's me." I answered almost dropping the phone on the floor. "No everything is just fine for a fucked up situation."

"Why were you screaming?" I felt that she'd left it a little late in the day to be so concerned about my wellbeing.

"Oh I just gave Robbie a fricking full on flash of my entire anatomy that's all. Why the hell didn't you know about her Jessica?" I asked annoyed at the fact that she was the one who set this ordeal up.

"Well maybe when all this was being discussed I must have been too pissed to have taken the information in. You know what I'm like Sarah, get me in a pub and I'm the best customer they'll have all night. But if it's any consolation she is rather stunning isn't she, for a masculine looking woman I mean. Anyway why is she there? At your place I mean, I thought you were going to tell her to fuck off, just like we planned."

"Jessica you have no idea do you. You also missed the fact that she was informed she'd be residing with me indefinitely. That's what sealed the deal for her." This whole scam had back fired on me and I only had myself to blame.

"Oh shit Sarah you are in a pickle. It is funny tho." She giggled, but that's because this wasn't happening to her.

"Do you have any idea Jessica how this is going to affect me? My parents like to call round at any time unannounced, my Chinese takeout evenings in with my other mates will have to be put on hold for a while. Just get your bloody arse round here and help me out. I have to come up with a cover story. You have to help me Jessica!" I was beginning to feel uneasy at the thought that I was to be a laughing stock to all my friends once they found out what I'd done so a simple lie would have to be put in place.

"Ok I'll be round in about half an hour. Or would you two like some alone time together? I bet she thinks you're a right little hottie." And so the jokes begin at my expense.

"She's not even gay, is she?" I hadn't even considered that fact, but what if she was and I'd just turned her on, what if she thought that I was coming on to her, does she think that I'm gay? Shit too many questions so little time.

I slammed the phone down and caught a glimpse of my reflection in the mirror and I couldn't believe she had been privy to my most intimate parts. But I do have a good body I thought. Maybe she liked what she saw; I secretly hoped that she did anyway. I put on a

Chapter One: For the Love of Immigration

small grey shoestring strap top, one of my sexiest, that allowed my nipples to protrude and if I leant forwards it showed off a little of what's not available, and I put on a pair of really short shorts. I had no idea what I was even thinking, dressing so seductively, but I felt compelled into doing it. I entered the lounge feeling a little nervous; the thought of her being privy not only to my womanhood but also my private collection. Had she seen any of my sex toys, my slutty knickers oh god my porno? I noticed how everything looked immaculately clean my mess had been picked up and placed into a neat tidy pile and an aroma of coffee wafted in from the kitchen.

"Do you take sugar?" She called out.

"Umm no thanks I just have cream in it!" I replied and sat comfortably on the sofa watching her get acquainted with the contents of the kitchen.

She made her way over with a tray consisting of three cups of coffee and a plate of cookies. "I made one for your friend too; I take it she is on her way here?" She queried as she placed everything down on the table in front of me.

"Oh yes she'll be here any moment, I've asked her to come over and help me, I mean us." I remarked quickly trying to act as if I was in control of the situation and knew what I was talking about.

I didn't know whether to sit down or stand up, or make myself busy. This was my home yet I felt awkward and strange and completely invaded. The knock on the door couldn't have come soon enough.

CHAPTER TWO

BUTTERFLIES IN MY STOMACH

*T*wo coffees and a cookie later the three of us were still sitting on the carpet next to the coffee table, trying to think up some reasonable convincing story of who Robbie was and why she was going to be hanging around for a while. After all she had never been mentioned to any of my colleagues before, so why would I have a stranger staying with me and a Canadian one at that?

"I know what we can say!" Jessica shouted out excitedly. "Robbie can be my distant cousin and ended up staying with you because my place is far too small to house a guest. So you are doing me a favour, as after all I am your best friend." Right at this moment in time that statement could quite possibly be debateable.

"Ok I think that could work, no one would question how we met each other. Yes I think we'll use that." I was grateful for any cover story right now and this one seemed like a simple one that no one would even question.

At that moment there was a loud knock on the door. It was Jake my so called fuck buddy of a lousy wanna be boyfriend. Every time I see him I keep meaning to dump his ungrateful ass but for some reason we always end up shagging.

"What are you doing here Jake?" I asked trying to prevent him from entering.

"Hi Sarah I know I should have called first but I need to speak to you in private do you have a moment? I'm off on a business trip tomorrow and it could end up being away for a few weeks." He peered in through the gap and could see that I had guests.

"We better talk in my bedroom come on through." I suggested, wondering what on earth was so important that he needed to talk about it now.

"Oh hi Jake you look good!" Jessica said in a rather school girlish tone and then proceeded to make herself look adorable by batting her eyelashes at him.

"Whatever." He replied coldly as his glance towards her was like it was too much of an effort to make.

"This is Robbie, Jessica's cousin. She's going to be staying with me for a while." He was going to be my first victim to my lie: My fingers were crossed and I was nearly peeing in my pants hoping that I sounded convincing enough.

"Hi Jake, it's a pleasure to meet you." She spoke softly and held her hand out to greet him. I could see her scanning him with those amazing blue eyes, like she was reading his every movement.

"Jake, this way please." I suggested rather impatiently. "Surely you know the way to my bedroom by now this had better be worth it."

When we entered my room I sat down on the bed and informed him that he was actually interrupting me in something important and that I had to get back to it.

"Little Jake would like to come out and play with little Sarah." He joked around trying to caress me and tugged at my clothes in attempt to remove them for his own pleasure.

"Is that why you came here Jake, for a shag before leaving to go on a trip? The answer is no; I won't let you use me like that anymore. It stops right now." My temper was growing pretty fast with him and to be honest I was also growing sick of seeing his pain in the ass face.

"No not just for that! There is a chance that I'll get promoted after this trip and if I do I need to be just like the big boys. They are all married with kids and have a great social life together outside of work. The thing is they are a close knit network and don't trust too many people outside of their loop. I need to fit in and be a part of that, I also told a small white lie; they think we're married. So how about it Sarah, what have you got to lose?" He seemed quite sure of himself and that I would instantly say yes to this.

"My fucking sanity for sure." I replied in disgust. "Do you think so little of me that you thought I would even consider saying yes?"

I noticed he was holding a pink velvet box in his hand and realised that he really was a piece of scum. He actually thought I would do it. I could feel myself building up into an angry frenzy and I really wanted to slap him at this point.

"Look give it some thought whilst I'm away you can even hold on to the ring just to get a feel for it if you like." As he presented me with the box opened and displaying an amazing diamond ring he saw that I was already wearing a gold band on my finger."Is that new? I haven't seen you wear it before." How the hell he had gotten this far in life I'll never know.

"Oh it's nothing; I umm sometimes put it on to keep unwanted attention away when I'm out with the girls. You know what ass holes are like when they've had too much to drink; can't keep they're fucking wondering hands off me." I had actually forgotten that I was wearing it. The strangest thing is that it felt natural to be there, like it was a part of me. Whilst he was staring at it I removed it from my finger and placed it on my dresser and almost immediately I wanted to put it back on. I needed Jake to really piss off now so that I could sort my shit of a life out so I urged him to go back into the lounge so we could join the others.

Jessica had helped herself to a bottle of my favourite Shiraz and had taken it out onto the balcony where she was smoking a cigarette quite fiercely and I had a feeling that she had gone a little cold on me. Robbie was standing by the opened doorway talking to her. The image of her leaning in towards the glass pane and the curtains slightly shimmering from the breeze that flowed through gave me butterflies in my stomach. Why had I got these strange feelings when I was around her? She fascinated me making me more intrigued each time I looked at her not wanting to divert my eyes anywhere else. She turned and walked towards me holding out her glass of wine as if to offer it to me and as she did everything felt like it was in slow motion and I was able to absorb each tiny detail. Her hands; slender but strong looking, her face; masculine and beautiful, her smile; amazing and pleasing.

"Here you are Sarah." She said losing her smile and gaining a frown. "I think you might need this."

I stepped out onto the balcony and told Jessica about Jake's ridiculous offer of marriage and she seemed a little disinterested and faced the opposite way from me. Her reaction surprised me but before I was able to quiz her on it Jake announced that he had to leave and she quickly jumped at the chance to be available and offered to give him a lift. Her eagerness to leave didn't go unnoticed with me.

"I'll see you tomorrow night at the club Sarah, bye Robbie I'll probably see you again soon, c'mon Jake lets go." She left moodily without saying what I had done to annoy her.

I looked at Robbie and asked her if I had just had a falling out with Jessica as I was slightly at a loss at what had just happened.

"I think your friend is in love with your boyfriend, it seems like she has been for a while from what I can gather." She calmly informed me then drank a huge swig of her wine.

"No fucking way!" I protested. "How dare you assume you know my friend; you don't know what she feels about things. Jake isn't even the type of guy she goes after, and she's heard me say numerous times what a jerk he is. God you're so full of shit! Fuck off! Just fucking fuck off!" I took a huge swig of my wine spilling some down my chin which just intensified my fury.

"I was only repeating what Jessica told me Sarah! I'm sorry that I hurt your feelings it was unintentional." She raised her eyebrows in surprise at my reaction then tried to comfort me but I pulled away from her not believing the lies that were coming out of her mouth.

I felt a little intimidated, there was no way that Jessica could have a thing for Jake, not like that anyway. He's a bore and a complete twat and kisses his boss's arse far too much. I'm sure I would have sensed it. No a total stranger couldn't know her better than me; she's absolutely got it wrong and as for Jake he's so out of my life from now on.

I noticed that my shoes had been removed from their usual place by the entrance door; it may be a petty thing to most people I thought, but I can always rely on my old favourites to be right where I last threw them.

"Did you move my shoes at all Robbie?" I asked rather sternly knowing that she had put them somewhere that she preferred much to my annoyance.

"Oh yes I saw that they were in the way of the door so I put them in your closet, whilst you were in the shower. Was that not the right thing to do?" She asked, wondering why I was so bothered by this.

"Oh for fuck sake!" I snorted loudly. "Please don't move my things around. I like to live in a chaotic mess, that's me, it's who I am. They stay by the door in future, that's if it's not too much to ask of you in my own home." My outburst was pathetic but I was feeling invaded and I wanted to gain back the control of my kingdom before she completely stole my identity.

"I'm sorry once again Sarah." She said sadly. "Next time I will remember to leave your shoes wherever you kick them off. It won't happen again, I promise." She seemed defeated by my outrage and I knew that I had overreacted to the situation.

"Please do! And start looking for somewhere else to live will you, this is my home and my life and I want it back!" I shouted hysterically at her not giving a damn if I had hurt her feelings.

As she walked away from me towards her room I suddenly noticed how much of a fit built body she had. The muscles in her arms were well toned with strong definition and her butt cheeks were really tight and firm and showed off quite nicely in her jeans. She must work out a lot to keep that shape, I thought to myself. As I stared at her in an admiring manner she caught me looking, which was slightly embarrassing, so I quickly picked up a magazine that had been placed on the table next me, then hopped onto the couch and remained acting as casual as I possibly could. Moments later she emerged from her room carrying a black jacket and a wallet.

"I'm going out for a while, you could probably do with some time for yourself." she said looking at me as if she was waiting for my approval. "I'm not sure how long I'll be but do you need me to bring you anything back?" She was reaching out to me as best she could under the circumstances.

I raised my eyes and looked directly at her pretending that I had been deeply interested in a story that the magazine had printed. I casually replied; "Oh no, I don't think so thanks."

"Alright then by the way I don't think that that is your kind of magazine Sarah; it's one of mine; for my type if you know what I mean."

As I looked down at the article that I was so flakily reading I was faced with a picture of two women laying seductively together on a rather large bed and entwined around their naked bodies was a deep purple silk sheet just covering enough skin to keep it from being a porno shot. Although in my eyes it actually was. I wanted to stare at it longer; to capture the image in my mind but now was not the right time. Why did I get the feeling that whenever I was around her something embarrassing tended to happen to me?

"So anyway do you have a spare key or should I just knock when I get back?" She stood there waiting patiently and I felt superior to her needs.

"I think there's a spare key on the shelf behind you." I told her as I pointed in its general direction. "It's the one with the photo of me hugging my so called best friend Jessica on the beach. Look I'm sorry that I lost my temper with you, I was just venting. Please don't take it personally I really didn't mean to offend you ok." Whenever I had an argument with Jessica we would say some awful hurtful things to each other but we always made it up straight away: Robbie would have to understand my ways if she was going to stay with me.

"That's ok Sarah, I think under the circumstances you have behaved particularly calm. You have every right to be frustrated with me." What was it about this woman that whatever she said seemed to be calming and reassuring she was like a fucking martyr.

Just as she left I grabbed a bag of toffee popcorn from the kitchen and made myself comfortable on the couch and switched on the TV.

There wasn't much on so I began to channel surf for the next two hours. I was absolutely bored stiff and I found myself wondering where Robbie had gone to and who was she with. I was actually beginning to miss her. She'd been invited to stay in my home and I hardly knew anything about her. I started to wonder who all those people were at our so called ceremony and what are all her friends like? Does she have a job? Is she a violent murderer? Or a drug addict? Or worse than that a sex addict who's waiting for me to fall asleep so that she can have her wicked way with me when I'm defenceless, not that that was a bad idea I thought. What was it about her that made me secretly want to flaunt myself at her? My mind was starting to work overtime having all of these crazy thoughts enter my head. I had allowed this situation to happen to me when I should have just said no! But I think that because I have always had such low moral standards about myself and never being in a serious relationship that meant more than two caramel toffees to me, I didn't realise that I could possibly start to like this person. The feeling of butterflies would flutter through my body every time I thought of her and I started to get slightly emotional when I realised that I was actually missing her company.

The security monitor caught my attention when a female figure, my new neighbour, stepped out of the lift closely followed by a male who was clearly impatient with his eager intensions. They were both drunk and disorderly and instead of opening her front door they decided that it was a good idea to get down to business leaning against it. He got down on his knees and slowly pulled her knickers down her legs. Then failing to care whether any of her neighbours were to be confronted with this sight she lifted up her skirt and allowed him to perform oral sex on her. I couldn't watch anymore of this slutty show and needed to clear my mind. Thinking about my situation I began to wonder what kind of person Robbie actually was, so sneaking into her room I found myself snooping amongst her personal possessions. She didn't have too much; just a few photos one in particular that caught my eye; she was with another woman rather elegant

Chapter Two: Butterflies in My Stomach 21

in appearance and their embrace was quite intimate. Was this her past lover, a present girlfriend? She had a good taste in fashion tho as all her gear was designer labels and her underwear drawer contained only boxer shorts and there were no bras in sight. She possessed very little to give me any information on her background.

I remembered that I had put her ring on my dressing table and felt a sudden urge to put it back on so I ran to the bedroom and picked it up and as I was admiring it I could see that there was an inscription written on the inside. It said; thank you. This was touching: she had thanked me from the beginning and I hadn't noticed. I replaced it back on my finger and then began to dance around the apartment like a drunken ballerina, stopping at every mirror that I past to see the shiny spectacle glisten back at me. Whilst I was twirling around I heard Robbie turn the key in the lock. My face was a little reddened and I was breathing at a heavy pace and it was difficult to calm it down before she noticed.

"Hi you're home already." I said followed by a large gulp of air." Did you have nice time out?"

"Yes I did thanks, are you ok Sarah? You seem to have some difficulty breathing." She grabbed a bottle of water from the fridge and threw it over to me.

"Oh yes I'm fine just doing some umm exercising. Yes that's it I was working out. You know; the way my type does." I smiled at her defiantly and drank several gulps of water.

"Touché my friend." She replied, acknowledging my sense of wit.

"So I was thinking would you like to go out for dinner tonight, my treat. I'd like to make up for being such a cow to you. I don't usually treat my guests like this." I was genuinely sorry for the way that I had treated her and I had realised that she had been thrown into this situation without too much information herself.

"Why Sarah, are you sure you want to be seen out with my type; you know; a lesbian!" She said in a joking manner and slung her jacket over the back of the sofa: with my approval of course.

We both giggled together and I was getting a sensation that I had never felt before. A feeling of wanting to know what this person is about, I was intrigued by her mannerism, and I found that I actually had time to listen to her while she was talking. I hung on every word that she spoke and I noticed how her eyes sparkled and looked full of life.

"So what should I wear?" She asked looking down at her footwear. "Don't forget, us dykes only wear DM's you know."

"Go as you normally would I suppose." I replied wondering what sort of attire she would be seen out in. "I'd like to be out with the real you." This was exciting and new to me I'd never been on a date with a woman before.

"So I see you've put my ring back on." She so politely pointed out.

"Oh well, I was just trying it on to see how it felt. It's different from the other rings I tend to wear." I replied feeling like I'd just got busted. "So let's get ready and meet back here in about thirty minutes if that's alright with you? Let's see who can get ready the fastest."

"It's game on lady." She answered in a challenging manner.

We both raced to our rooms and I could feel the excitement building up inside me as I searched for something hot and sexy to wear. Everything looked so neat and in order. Robbie had done a really nice job of tidying my messy stuff up. I found a really sexy white halter neck see through top that I had completely forgotten about and paired it up with a short tight black skirt, I looked fucking hot, what lesbian wouldn't be attracted to this little hottie?

I arrived in the lounge first and waited patiently on the sofa constantly checking myself out in the mirror that was hanging above the fireplace.

Robbie's entrance into the room gave me goose bumps all over. She looked absafuckinglutely stunning in a white waist coat and tight fitting jeans and she wasn't joking about the DM boots. I had been put under her spell and I liked it.

"Well do I pass?" She asked as she gave me a slow twirl to show off, she looked hotter than I did.

"You have excelled my expectations." I informed her. "And I like the tattoo of butterflies on your shoulder, is there a reason for that design?" It was a simple design but very attractive.

"Oh the reason I had that done, is for freedom. Butterflies are free to fly anywhere they want and I compared them to someone I have known for a long time." She looked a little sad by this permanent reminder so it must mean something really important to her.

"That's nice to have such an intense meaning I think." I wondered who she meant by that comment and just smiled sweetly at her as we readied to leave on our date.

CHAPTER THREE

MY FIRST GAY CLUB

We ended up at my favourite Italian restaurant that I liked to frequent every now and then and we sat by a window that over looked a cobbled stone street and was in close proximity to the shop on the opposite side that sold old fashioned sweets. We placed an order of a large ham and pineapple pizza to share between us and a bottle of red wine that had a chocolaty blackcurrant note to it. There was a small candle flickering in the middle of the table which gave an orange reflective glow to Robbie's silhouette showing off her unique bone structure, it definitely created a romantic ambiance.

The conversation was polite and light hearted to begin with, but I wanted to delve in and learn more information about my new wife. More likely my usual need to be a nosey hag was itching to surface. She informed me that she is twenty nine years old and that her family are still living in Canada. The actual reason for her needing to stay in England was that a really close friend of hers was extremely ill and she didn't want to leave her alone. Not that her friend didn't have other friends, but their relationship was a far closer one than just friendship. The only way she could stay at such short notice was to marry quickly and be sponsored to stay under the spousal application. That's where I came in and the only personal information that she was given on me was my name and that I was willing to do this for her. And also that I might possibly be gay, as at my age most women have been married at some point or other in their lives. She had been out to visit with her sick friend this afternoon to let her know that she was safe and that I wasn't a psychopath. Her friend had enjoyed their visit as she had gotten a good laugh out of all of this.

The conversation turned deeper into a meaningful interest and we were both hanging on every word we both spoke and listening quite intensely. It was here when I noticed her lips were full and sensual looking and I began to day dream about what it would be like to be locked in a kiss with them and how would it feel to have them touch my skin and tease my senses. Something was definitely stirring inside me and I was feeling ok with it.

I felt compelled to tell her about my life history, right from where I grew up in Bristol as a little girl to how I had met Jessica and we both moved to London in our early twenties, and how I had worked my way up the ladder to become the manager of a clothing store that sold designer wear.

We also discussed the situation that we were in and decided that it would be ok for her to stay at my pad for the duration of the marriage. It just made more sense, and I think deep down I was glad of this arrangement, I had a compelling urge to keep her close in my life.

"Well living arrangements can wait for now." I suggested. "Let's go clubbing! I'm up for a good night on the tiles. Besides you look hot and I look sexy so I think we should make the most of it, what do you think?" The correct answer is yes, please say yes.

"Ok I know a cool place we can go to, it's not far from here. Trust me you'll love it." She winked at me then took a bite from her pizza dropping chunks of pineapple onto the tablecloth; strangely it came across as a sexy move.

"Oh I didn't know there was a club in this area, is it new?" I couldn't place where a club could possibly be as I thought I knew the area well enough.

"No Sarah it's been open for a long time, it's just not the kind of place you would have thought to frequent before. So you have probably walked past it many times and not realised it was there."

We paid our bill and made our way to the club by walking through a small alley way and then down a narrow street. The fresh air made me feel a little light headed and I was getting giggly for no apparent reason. Robbie was right; I had walked past this place on many occasions and never paid it any attention. Probably because there were steps leading from the curb side downwards towards a plain doorway. There was absolutely nothing to suggest that there was a club behind it. There was just a small neon sign lit up with the words, The Pink Rainbow. Once inside I could see that it wasn't a very big place but it was packed with women of all descriptions. Robbie led me to the bar making sure that I stayed close behind her, as apparently I was fresh meat ready for the dykes to pounce on. They should be so lucky. I noticed that there were a lot of women wearing beater tops which enabled them to show off their muscles as if there was a competition going on between them. I must admit it was a turn on to see, and the more girlie types seemed to be hanging around them vying to get their attention. It was exactly the same as the straight world, the hunt, the capture, the prize, except there were no male partakers in this lifestyle.

Robbie ordered us two bottles of beers; she said it looked sexy to see a woman drink straight from the bottle. The music was booming and the atmosphere was full of loud voices all trying to hear each speak other over it.

I took a swig of my beer and watched the women on the dance floor. Seeing how gently and seductive a woman could touch and caress another woman was a major turn on to me, and I found myself studying their motions hard. When I looked back at Robbie I saw that she was watching me, to see my reactions to the displays of affection that were being put on show.

"Would you like to dance?" Her invitation was welcoming and I quickly took her up on it.

"Sure I would!" I replied. "Let's shake it baby!"

"Then take my hand sexy lady and show me what you're made of." She requested as we both made our way through the crowd and on to the dance floor.

We stood close enough to each other that I could feel her breath on my face, and she smelt of fresh light tones that were starting to drive me crazy with excitement. Her hands were holding my waist gently and she had a constant smile on her face. I placed my arms

Chapter Three: My First Gay Club

loosely around her neck and she pulled me in closer to her where our eyes met and were locked on to each other as we danced slow and seductively.

"So what type of girl do you normally go for Robbie, blondes, Brunettes, girlie types?" I was inquisitive to know her taste and how she would choose her girlfriends and did she possibly find me attractive?

"Ok Sarah, I don't think you quite understand what I'm about. It's not like picking a type and going for the kill, for me. I prefer to get to know a person and let a relationship build itself naturally to a romantic level. That way there's less drama as there tends to be a lot of that in lesbian land. I do like to tread carefully with women." Well she was certainly quite the opposite type of person to me; I couldn't even name half the guys I'd slept with.

"So would I be your type? I asked, hoping that she'd say that I was the most amazing, attractive, sexiest woman she had ever met.

With a small giggle she said; "Just dance with me Sarah; let's not talk about me anymore I feel like my life stories could bore the hell out of you."

After downing several bottles of beer, hopefully looking sexy as I did it, we decided that it was time to call it a night. My shoes were killing me, but I was still high with excitement as we made our way back home. It was a really warm night, or rather morning so we chose to go on foot, as it was only a fifteen minute walk. I must have tripped over at least three times, trying not to look a fool, but with each fall Robbie was quick to react and catch me. I liked the touch of her hands as she pulled me back up and I made sure that I brushed up against her on more than one occasion.

CHAPTER FOUR

BOOBS BUMS AND THE NAKED TRUTH

*T*he sound of a dog barking in the distance and birds singing happily woke me up. It was already midday and as I sat up I tried to focus on the fake Van Gough print I had so proudly hung on my wall. My head was throbbing and my mouth was extremely dry then I came to the realisation that I had passed out on the couch, and as I came to a little more, I could see that my skirt had wrapped itself up towards my waist. But not only had I passed out, I had actually done it with Robbie lying next to me. Her waist coat had been removed to reveal a plain white up lifter bra, this showed off her cleavage and I could see that her stomach muscles were well toned. But it was where my hand had been placed that concerned me. It was parked right on top of her left breast. I jumped up quickly; rather too quickly, and lost my balance, causing me to trip over the coffee table and I ended up faced down on the ground with my arse on show for all to see.

A large bellow of; "Oh shit." shot from my mouth, causing Robbie to stir.

She shot up quickly and was surprised by my insane posture. "Oh, I see you wear sexy thongs. That's interesting!"

Then she got up and came to my rescue once again by hoisting me up and propping my bruised body or rather my bruised ego, onto the sofa.

"I'm so embarrassed." I said coyly whilst trying to pull my clothing back into its correct place.

"You don't have to be, I quite enjoyed the show. C'mon I'll make us some coffee." She said nonchalantly and gave me a friendly kiss on the top of my head.

"Robbie can I ask you a personal question, does this mean that I'm gay now? You know sleeping with you on the sofa and feeling

Chapter Four: Boobs Bums and the Naked Truth

you up like that? Have I crossed over?" I said with a slight stammer, as my mind was in torment with itself, one half saying don't be stupid, no fucking way, and the other half hoping that her answer would be, yeah full on babe, go gay for Robbie.

"No Sarah."She said with a loud laugh. "You are far too high maintenance to be a lesbian. And nothing untoward happened between us last night, I promise. I would never have taken advantage of you in your state. You were way too drunk. In fact you actually tried to come on to me and you pushed me down on to the sofa and jumped on top of me. That's how come we ended up there this morning; I didn't want to move you after you passed out."

She went off to make us some coffee and I could hear her laughing softly on the other side of the wall. Why was I constantly making a fool out of myself in front of her? I was beginning to come across as complete idiot, a far cry from the woman who held total control over her life just a few days ago. But my instincts were telling me I needed to impress her, get her attention somehow, and show her that I am a desirable woman even if I'm not gay!

She brought the coffees into the lounge and we sat next to each other on the couch sipping away at the hot steamy beverage; which by the way burnt the top of my mouth but I wasn't about to let her know that.

"Sarah will you just relax: Please!" She asked with a concerned look on her face. "I'm not that good that I can turn a straight girl gay over night! Everything is cool between us. Honest."

Just at that moment she put her hand on my arm and I saw sincerity in her eyes. So why was I feeling so disappointed that nothing had happened? I didn't want it to have, I think, but the feeling that she didn't even attempt to make out with me made me feel like I wasn't good enough to be a part of her world. To have the knowledge that she at least fancied me a little bit would have given me some sort of satisfaction in my confused state.

"Well Robbie I think I should pop into my place of work and check that everything is running smoothly without me." I said, as I pulled my arm away slowly from her welcomed grasp, although I wanted it to last forever.

"Ok, I'll go and visit my friend Kate, the one I told you about last night. I have to help tend to house work for her and do some shopping. She's still a bit on the week side at the moment. I'm just worried that she'll try to do too much on her own; the chemotherapy did take it out of her and I want to make sure she recovers properly."

"Sure that would be nice for her; I bet she enjoys your visits." I felt sorry for her friend but it must be very comforting for her having a friend like Robbie. "Well if you're interested I'm going out with friends tonight, you're more than welcome to join us if you like."

"Well if everything's good with Kate I'll try to join you." She seemed happy that I had offered her a place in my social life and I secretly hoped that she would be able to join us.

I wrote my number down on a paper napkin and handed it to her, then headed off to work. For the rest of the afternoon I found myself daydreaming about Robbie. She was almost in all of my thoughts. If I saw a customer try something on I'd think, ooh that would look good on Robbie, or, I wonder if Robbie likes Chinese food. I also started to remember what she had said about Jessica and Jake. Maybe she was right after all. The way that my best friend had left yesterday was disturbing and I needed to talk her to clear the air. If I was being honest with myself, I really didn't care that she fancied him. I had no use at all to have that jerk in my life; I just wished she could see him in the same light as I did then she would know what a useless dirt bag he was.

As the working day came to its end, there were no major sales to rejoice about. Bleach blue jeans seemed to have been the favourite purchases, along with a few gift cards but business in general was good. The walk home gave me time to reflect on the recent events from the last few days and how I'd enjoyed myself at the Pink Rainbow club. Robbie was probably the best thing that had happened to me in such a long time, and the need to quicken my pace as I got closer to home overwhelmed me. I found myself running towards the front door of my building and the excitement of seeing her; the thought of her waiting for my return rushed through me as I entered the hallway. For the first time I was happy to be home.

"Robbie!" I shouted out as I ran through the apartment. "Are you here? It's me Sarah I'm home."

There was no reply and the silence that greeted me was disappointing. Maybe she had to give Kate a lot more attention than she had expected to. I had to overcome my selfishness and remember that the world didn't just revolve around me so I turned on my CD player and the next song to come on was one of my favourite oldies from the sixties. My mood lifted in hearing this and I perked up enough to make getting ready to go out a more enjoyable experience. I chose one of my favourite dresses, a small black number that showed off every curve of my body, and I lay it out neatly on the bed. Stripping down to just my knickers, I boogied out into the hallway singing; totally out of key of course and without a care in the world. Using my hairbrush as my mike I got totally engrossed with the music and before I realised it, standing in front of me was Robbie. I hadn't heard her call out to me when she arrived home and I just froze like a bunny in headlights. This time I made no attempt to cover myself up and I let her have a full on glance of my almost naked slender figure. I had no idea what to do next so I looked directly into her eyes, searching for any signs of her wanting to touch me. I couldn't read her thoughts and tears began to well up in my eyes from the frustration and confusion of not having her in my arms, not being able to hold her, not being able to feel her, not being able to have her and not understanding why.

"Hey Sarah; are you alright?" She asked with a concerned voice. "Why are you crying?"

"Well I suppose I could lie to you and tell you that my eyeliner was irritating me because I'm allergic to it." I sobbed not caring that this was the most humiliating thing to ever have happened to me. "Or I could just be honest and ask you why don't you find me attractive, why haven't you made a move on me, am I that ugly to you?" I started to turn into a blubbering wreck, and shame was beginning to play a cruel role in my emotions.

"But I do find you attractive." She stated clearly. "I admire every inch of your body, your long legs that lead up to that cute mole sitting right on top of your thigh and your breasts are really teasing me right now, and your smile! Oh Sarah, how I want to kiss that beautiful smile you wear! So in answer to your question I do want to jump your bones." She paused; then after completing her study of my assets her eyes met mine.

We stopped dead in our exploration of each other and suddenly without warning I pounced towards her like an animal, not giving my action a second thought forcing her to drop her keys on the floor in order to receive my advances and with heavy emotional breathing we were interlocked in a passionate kiss.

I pressed my body hard against hers giving me access to feel her deep evocative breathing as she moved her hands up my back until she reached my hair and held my locks tight as if she never wanted to let me go. I pulled at the belt on her jeans and unfastened them to reveal a black pair of mini shorts peaking through the opened zip. Kissing her hard and fast, I lifted her top over her head and threw it onto the small table by the door almost knocking the vase of roses clear off it. Her breasts were large and firm, and I found myself kissing her up and down from her full lips, to her neck and then to the plump mounds of desirable flesh that greeted me. The passion was so strong between us, and seeing the bedroom door was open behind me, she lifted me up and carried me through, gently placing me on the bed and landing on top of me. She took complete control of the situation and before long I was writhing with excitement as I watched her remove the rest of her clothing. Her body was immaculate and I wanted whatever she was prepared to offer me. My eyes were focused on her mouth as she kissed my wrists and used her tongue to tickle my arms as she gently glided it up towards my neck. Then as she lightly nibbled downwards towards my breasts I bit my lower lip to control the sounds of ecstasy. She moved down lower, kissing my stomach and my inner thighs, and using both of her hands she gently parted my legs open. I could feel her warm breath just before her

Chapter Four: Boobs Bums and the Naked Truth

soft wet tongue stroked me. With light movements to begin with, she then gave a stronger more passionate motion that encouraged me to arch my body up so that I could receive her fully. My wildest fantasies couldn't have prepared me for this overwhelming feeling and I couldn't control myself any longer, and as I released my sexual build up on her I grabbed her hair and announced loudly with great pleasure that I was cumming. It was like the phoenix magnificently rising out of the flames. I could hardly catch my breath.

As my breathing slowed down I began to realise that I was at my most vulnerable, and to have given myself as freely as I did without any concerns, gave me an overwhelming surge of affectionate thoughts this was something that I had never experienced before!

I began to stroke her hair as she ran her fingers over my body with a light sensual touch, then kissing my stomach, she moved upwards towards my neck gently caressing my body with such seductive passion. It gave me a sensation of warmth and fulfilment and yummyness. We both stared into each other's eyes, possibly looking for recognition that everything was ok, and for a short moment silence fell between us.

"You have beautiful eyes." I whispered in her ear. "They're so blue and intriguing."

"Thank you, I get them from my mother's side." She replied and then kissed my forehead.

I wrapped my legs around her body and we held each other tightly and kissed with intense desire for what seemed to be an eternity. The thought of me repaying her the favour back entered my head; as I wanted her to experience the same euphoric pleasures that I had just gone through. So I started to kiss her neck and my hands wondered down to her fit well toned thighs. As I began to fondle, or more like fumble around, she gently took hold of my wrist and told me that I wasn't ready to proceed any further.

"Sarah I want you to enjoy what just happened between us." She spoke exceptionally calmly and I wasn't sure why she didn't want to proceed any further. "This was an amazing moment and I think we should take it to the next level at a later date."

"But I thought you wanted me to…."

She interrupted me with; "Oh my God, you on me would be a fantasy come true. But I want it to be right; I want you to be comfortable when you touch me."

"I suppose so; I have always been repulsed at performing oral sex. I've never been able to bring myself to do it." I was being honest with her but I had been repulsed at the thought of a penis in my mouth and never considered how I would feel eating a girl out. Actually I did come pretty close to it once tho. Last year whilst at an open air concert with Jessica we were sitting on a small grassy embankment waiting for the band to come on when a man in his fifties wearing a vest top and a white pair of cut off shorts that just covered his tackle walked right up in front of us, apparently looking for someone. He was that close to my face that if he'd had a hard on it would have been parked in my mouth enjoying the moment. Yuk!

She looked at me with deep concern and that's when she practically did a 360 on me.

"Sarah I don't know if we should have just done this." She said with a serious look on her face. "I mean I feel like I have just broken a golden rule. You're straight, you sleep with men and that's fine there's absolutely nothing wrong with that. You are a beautiful woman and every man must certainly lust after you! I'm so sorry but I think we've just crossed the line." She pulled the sheet up in an attempt to cover her body making me feel as though I was some kind of pervert.

"Hang on Robbie! I realise that I'm not exactly what you would portray as gay and that I'm not so experienced in your field, but I think we both wanted this to happen, something inside me has awakened and you're the cause of it." I was starting to feel scared by the way she was acting.

My voice became wobbly as I held back the tears of frustration. In one foul swoop I had experienced ecstasy along with humiliation and rejection.

Why was she making me feel as though I was to blame for her breaking her bloody golden rule? And if she felt so strongly about it then she bloody well should have kept her wondering hands off me.

"I have fantasised over you ever since I met you Robbie, does that not count for anything?" I cried out at her still horrified that she had completely rejected me.

"That's just it Sarah! I was a fantasy to you. You have to realise that I have met your kind before, first you get me all tied up with confused emotions that I can't breathe when I'm around you. Then you tease me with the way you touch your hair, the way you smile at me, the way you smell. Then you finish it off by giving me a full on show of that stunning body of yours. Twice! And yes it is stunning!" There was an air of annoyance in her reasoning and it felt as though she was trying to put me in my place.

"But I don't mean to Robbie and that truly was an accident with you seeing me naked." My plea seemed to be falling on deaf ears and the argument surely was one sided.

"Look Sarah, the reason why I'm so scared is that you are not ready for a serious relationship, especially a same sex one, that's why you agreed to marry a total stranger. I don't want to get hurt by you and I think we should forget about what just happened and maintain a professional relationship. I don't regret what we just did and I hope I meant more than just sex to you. We both have to be real here." How could she think that what just happened wasn't real and dismiss it so easily.

At that moment she got up off the bed, collected her clothes and left my room with nothing further to say. I was left feeling rather confused and greatly humiliated. Had this been the way that I'd behaved in the past every time I met a guy that I was so happy to fuck and then immediately get rid of? I had created a monster within myself, only to be bitten in the ass by an even bigger one! One that I had become so attracted to!

The hurt I felt soon turned into shame, and for the first time I saw myself as an ugly person that no one could possibly want. The tears poured out from me and I threw myself down on the bed, screaming into my pillow as I covered my face with it.

CHAPTER FIVE
LET'S GET IT ON

I must have cried myself to sleep as it was dark outside when I awoke. I knew my friends would be waiting for me to join them at the pub so I got dressed with very little enthusiasm, and made my way there. My eyes were still swollen and slightly red when I arrived but I was intent on speaking to Jessica. I thought that indulging myself in her problems I could momentarily take time out from thinking about my own.

Entering the pub I caught a quick glimpse of my reflection in the glass door and I wasn't impressed with what I saw as I would normally be the one little hottie of the group but now I just looked bedraggled and tired. Who knew that being married was exhausting?

Jessica was sitting at a large table with her friend Debs and they were joined by three other girls that worked with them at the office. They had invited themselves to tag along and they were already starting to get on the merry band wagon and being a little on the loud side. Jessica had already taken the liberty to order me a glass of wine in, but I wanted something a lot stronger than that to get me through the rest of the evening.

"It's my shout!" I called out rather eagerly and made my way to the bar and ordered us all a round of cocktails, which was well needed on my behalf.

"Well aren't you the party animal." Debs implied, as she quickly handed the drinks out to everyone.

"I phoned your apartment before you got here." Jessica informed me. "Robbie answered and she said you were on your way, she seemed reluctant to talk to me. Is everything alright Sarah? Your eyes are red. You've been crying haven't you?" She gave me a tissue that she found in her bag; it had a pink lipstick mark on it where she had blotted her lips earlier so I folded it over and used the corner to wipe away any remnants of mascara that had run down my face.

"Well sort of."I said trying to hide my eyes with a few strands of hair that were dangling. "I… I umm well; I just had a big fight with mum on the phone, that's all. It's nothing to get concerned about, I'm alright, honest." I crossed my fingers together under the table in hope that no one caught on to the fact that I had just told a big fat fib. Even though Jessica was my best friend it didn't feel right to inform her that Robbie had just gone down on me and then kicked me to the curb leaving me hurt and feeling used.

"Anyway what's happening with us?" I said in order to change the subject. "Things didn't seem right between us when you left yesterday."

"Yes I know. I've been meaning to tell you something for a while, please don't be angry with me with what I'm about to tell you. I'm in love with Jake! I have been since I first met him. Sarah I'm so sorry and I didn't set out to hurt you but I can't fight these feelings anymore. Please don't be mad with me." She had been brave enough and honest enough to tell me what she was feeling and I had to respect that.

I held my drink in the up as to make a toast and looked Jessica directly in her eyes. "Here's to best mates because without them we'd all be living a fucking boring life. And here's to my best mate Jessica and Jake making a go of it! Good luck girl you're gonna need plenty of it with that one!"

We chinked our glasses together and as we did Jessica toasted back. "And here's to Sarah finding the love of her life! God help him whoever he turns out to be."

We burst out laughing at the statements we had just made and gave each other a big hug to gain back the sincerity that we had before.

After drinking a few cocktails the girls that were sitting with us started to get a little on the rowdy side. Bitchy remarks were flying between them about other females in the pub. I asked Debs if we could ditch them before we went clubbing and she informed me that they were only acting in the same way that we usually did. Jessica must have told her all about our evenings out, else how would she know what I was like, I'd only met her once before, and that was for about five minutes, she had scarpered pretty quickly after my alliance to Robbie.

I felt sick seeing their ugliness on display like that and that in the past I had portrayed myself in that exact same manner. It was disgraceful behaviour.

"She looks like she's got two frozen peas shoved down her bra." The one girl bitched as she lifted her glass to her mouth in order not to be seen saying those words.

And the other girl leaned in towards her and replied with; "I wouldn't leave the house looking like that, she looks like a right dyke just look at those boots that she's wearing." That remark hit a nerve with me and as Jessica and Debs looked away with total embarrassment, it was then that I decided that I couldn't hold it in anymore.

"Why don't you just shut up?" I yelled straight in to their faces. "You three bitches had better piss off right now!"

I saw the look of naïve stupidity on their faces as they couldn't care less what anyone thought of them. I really didn't feel up to drinking with them anymore, so I arranged with Jessica to call her the next day and made my excuses, I said goodbye to Debs and that we should do this again without the drama. She agreed and said that next time she would bring her friend Jen with her because I was very similar in my ways.

I decided to take my time walking home, checking out the sale items in the store window displays, and making a mental note to go back tomorrow and try on a pair of sling backs that I quite fancied. A bridal shop caught my attention with beautiful gowns perfectly on show. A sinking feeling dwelled in the pit of my stomach and broke the dreamy like moment. Maybe I was never meant to be the blushing bride walking down the aisle and live a happy ever after with prince charming, I thought.

Chapter Five: Let's Get it On

I had no idea what to expect upon my return home, it was late and I was too exhausted to carry on arguing with Robbie. The apartment was in darkness when I arrived back, and calling out her name to see if she was in I received no response. I tapped on her bedroom door and asked if I could come in, but still no reply. Disappointment surrounded me, as always being a person in constant control of my life I had turned into a blubbering flake.

With tormented emotions I went and lay down on the sofa and ended up watching a soppy love story on the TV. It gave me a good reason to burst into tears as I had absolutely no one that I could to turn to. Being a lonely loser didn't suit me and it sucked big time as far as I was concerned. A few glasses of wine and a bag of crisps later I managed to gather my senses together and began to reminisce over the hot sex I'd had earlier and I could still feel Robbie's full lips pressing hard against mine. I was hungry for more of that. I snuggled up to a pillow and wrapped my arms around it pretending it was Robbie cuddling me back when I heard the front door open. In walked Robbie and unknowingly she walked straight past me and into her room. She didn't even know I was lying there all alone and feeling scared. I waited for a few moments and when she turned her light off I crept quietly along the hallway to my room softly closing the door behind me.

I climbed into my bed still fully clothed as I was too depressed to bother to change and as I started to drift off I heard a light tapping noise on my door. It was Robbie asking if I was still awake, my heart jumped with excitement as I heard her whisper.

"Come in," I said: my voice was croaky from all the crying that I'd done and I quickly wiped my eyes with the back of my hand so she couldn't see the evidence. My heart started to race and a feeling of euphoria came over me as she walked into the room.

"Sarah, are you ok?" She asked in a soft caring tone. "I'm sorry for walking out on you like that, it was wrong of me and especially with it being your first time with a woman. I feel like such a shit. It kills me to be in that room when I know you're in here. I know you're going to break my heart Sarah Niles, but I ache for you, I can't stop thinking about you, about how you feel, how you smell, how you taste. So I suppose it's a chance I have to take."

I looked up at the masculine silhouette standing in the doorway. Her facial expressions were hidden in the shadows but I did know that she was being sincere with me. My heart melted like butter on hot pancakes and I confirmed my feelings with her.

"I want you more than anyone I've ever known. I've changed my ways in this short space of time, I have really changed! I began to get mentally involved with you as soon as I met you, and now you fill every thought in my mind. I have been going crazy not knowing what happened between us earlier. What the hell happened?" I sat up and busied myself by fluffing the pillows behind me.

"I've been hurt badly in the past and I don't take relationships lightly and the way I see it is that you're the kind of person to toss people aside when you get bored with them. I didn't know if I could face going through all of that turmoil again. I think what I'm trying to say is; I need you to be patient with me as I with you." It occurred to me that she was the deep thinking kind of girl who needed simplicity and honesty in her life and I was hoping that I was the one who could give her that, now that I was the new Sarah Niles; the girl with a big heart.

"Shush, now climb in." I suggested lifting the duvet up as an invitation for her to join me.

She stripped off her clothes slowly, knowing that I could only see the outline of her in the darkness. It was a very seductive gesture that had my fullest attention and I was mesmerised by the display that she put on.

She slid into bed and lay beside me. Her hand brushed up against my thigh in a slow sensual motion. As we kissed, she pushed her tongue into my mouth using soft long strokes. The intensity of just that one act had me writhing up against her body. She gently lifted my dress up above my waist, shortly followed by removing my knickers. Her hands were warm and soft and gentle, and she knew

Chapter Five: Let's Get it On

just how to use them on me. She paid particular attention to touching me between my thighs, teasing me before she entered me. I could feel the shape of her breasts pressing down on my chest as she thrust at my insides over and over again and it wasn't long until she brought me to climax.

My body was spent and I was both nervous and excited at the whole situation and I knew she could sense my enjoyment and kissed me hard as if hungry for my soul. Something had changed inside me as I had never given myself to anyone as freely as I had given myself to her.

It was now my turn to pleasure her, and at first I felt extremely awkward. I started off by kissing her neck and using long strokes with my tongue then I moved down towards her breasts. They were firm and well rounded and tasted of sweet body odour. I massaged her nipples with my tongue making them erect, and I could hear her breathing become deeper and slower as I moved further down to between her legs. Using a soft slow motion I kissed her inner thighs, and then I had my first taste of her, which reminded me of sweet pineapple. I had no idea if I was hitting the right spot but I could tell that she was enjoying it. Then she put both of her hands on my head and pulled me in closer to her as she began to writhe with pleasure. She let out a long groan and then relaxed her body as she relished in her enjoyment. I felt ecstatic that I had given her the same pleasure that I had had. This had been the best sexual experience of my life and as we fell asleep in each other's arms I knew I was going to have sweet dreams that night.

The bond grew stronger between us and the next few days were filled with more sexual lustful encounters. Not one room was spared the escape of our naked bodies being captivated in joined excitement. We had become sex maniacs with each other and my fondness for Robbie was developing into a mature harmony. I hadn't felt this happy in ages as I was finally able to enjoy what it felt like to be in a cozy relationship.

CHAPTER SIX

BITTER SWEET ENCOUNTERS

*R*obbie was visiting Kate today and had asked me to go with her. I was a little on the nervous side as this was the first time I was to meet one of her friends.

"Don't worry Sarah." She assured me. "Kate already likes you. I've told her loads about you and she can't wait to meet you so that she can put a face to all the stories I've told her." She put her arm around my shoulder and pulled me in close giving me the assurance that I was already a part of her social network.

Kate's house stood in the middle of a terrace row, and the red front door led directly from the curb. The house itself stood proudly and occupied three levels from the ground up and was white in colour with large windows allowing the natural light to flow through. Robbie had her own key so that she could let herself in, more for Kate's convenience, rather than her own.

As we entered the hallway I heard a soft spoken, almost bordering on the posh side, voice call out; "Is that you Robbie?"

"Yes Kate." She answered sweetly. "We're both here!"

"Come in; come in, how wonderful to see you both." She commented in a welcoming manner.

As I walked through the doorway I was faced with an elegant looking woman sitting on the couch and smiling contentedly. She was the same woman in Robbie's photo.

"Hi! You must be Sarah. I've heard so much about you. Don't worry it's all been good." She so quickly pointed out.

"Is there anything you need me to do for you Kate?" Robbie asked and began to pick up yesterday's newspapers from the coffee table ready to throw out.

"Well you can get the champagne out. We have something to celebrate today; I got the all clear from the Doctor this morning." Her smile was beaming and tears of joy began to roll down her face.

Robbie let out a gasp of relief and gave Kate a giant hug. They held their embrace for a few minutes and then Kate said; "Get the champagne out it's in the fridge and there's also some snacks on the side if you're hungry."

As Robbie disappeared into the kitchen Kate told me that no one had ever stolen Robbie's heart like I had and that maybe I was the one to finally settle down with her. Whilst we were talking I heard the front door open. A woman with jet black hair and a slender build walked in. She had a Cleopatra look about her; quite stunning if you liked that type.

"This is Jen, Jen this is Sarah, Robbie's wife." Kate patted on the sofa enticing me to sit next to her so that she could get a better look at me.

"So you're the one, are you?" Jen remarked in a dismissive manner.

"Hi it's nice to meet you Jen." I replied as pleasantly as I could given the fact that she had just spoken to me quite rudely.

"Likewise I suppose." She snapped back and then slumped into the armchair and picked at the grapes in the bowl next to her that were obviously meant for Kate. "So you agreed to go ahead with this ridiculous scam then?"

Before I could answer Robbie walked back in holding three glasses of bubbly and then came to a sudden halt. She looked completely horrified as she stared at Jen.

"What the hell are you doing here?" She yelled passing out the glasses quite forcibly.

"I'm sorry Robbie." Kate spoke with great empathy and I sensed she hadn't planned on letting the two women cross paths just yet. "Jen has been so good to me lately, she's really helped me out a lot and I can't rely on you solely."

"But that's why I'm here!" Robbie answered back with a look of despair on her face.

"Umm hello; I am still in the room you know." Jen's contempt showed as she rolled her eyes and then mimicked Robbie.

"Oh just shut up Jen! I don't want to hear you, look at you or speak to you. You're a walking nightmare." Robbie snapped at her. "Kate I'm really sorry that I lost my temper like that. Maybe we should leave and catch up with you tomorrow."

Jen stood up and walked over to the doorway and said in an extremely sarcastic manner; "You don't have to go on my account ladies, I'll go and sit in the garden and count the God damn clouds if I have to. Robbie forever the protector, you were never like that with me!"

As Robbie verbally stuck it to this woman, I felt a surge of unease run through my veins. What had this woman done to create such hatred? I sensed that there was something that went on between them, something deep and sinful. This woman was so stunning in her looks that I'm sure she knew that she could have anyone she wanted. Maybe she had possessed Robbie with her lustful wickedness.

She walked over to Kate and handed her a book that she had gone out to buy especially for her, and then casually made her way to the sanctuary of the garden.

"Oh god Kate why her; after all the hurt and lies that she's caused, why is she still hanging around?" Robbie was beside herself as she pleaded with Kate and I felt awkward not being privy to their secret.

"Let's not do this now Robbie, please, not in front of Sarah. Anyway let's change the subject I want to know how married life is treating you two." She smiled and sipped a small amount of champagne from her glass then encouraged us to do the same.

Oh God I wanted to tell her that sex with Robbie was the most amazing I'd ever had, but talking about my sexual encounters to another woman, ooh no way.

"Oh everything's great." Announced Robbie; "In fact it's better than that. Sarah's a really interesting person to hang around with." My opinion differed slightly on that fact, after all; we as in me and Robbie had a tremendous amount in common, the kitchen floor, the

Chapter Six: Bitter Sweet Encounters

bathroom, the bedroom, the sofa. We hadn't seen too much of the outside world and only my stories with limited information had been made available to Robbie. I didn't feel that Kate would find our intimacy interesting.

I felt myself blush, as all I could think about was the fantastic sex we'd been having. We had been talking for most of the afternoon about how Kate and Robbie first met, and how they had vacated together, and how I had spent my past, although I left quite a lot of info out of that conversation. I didn't want them being privy to my raunchy past like that. But I couldn't stop thinking about Jen sitting in the garden all this time, and wondering what the past history was between her and Robbie. Feelings of jealousy crept into my head and being the outsider in this was becoming most uncomfortable. In fact I had no knowledge at all of Robbie's past conquests. I needed to know more and my attention was ebbing towards thoughts of talking to Jen.

So I made an excuse that I needed to use the wash room and then I would go and put the glasses in the dishwasher so that Robbie and Kate could have a personal chat. But as soon as I left the room I headed straight for the garden where I found the little minx sitting at a small table, hogging a bottle of red wine and smoking a cigarette very seductively. I could see that her eyes were fixated on me as I approached.

"Hi, care to join me for one?" She offered holding the bottle in the air. "So have they sent you out here so that they can have some alone time together? You do know that they used to be an item before you came along don't you? Robbie has always been into Kate, but it was Kate that broke it off because of her illness. She didn't know if she was going to survive or not, so she spared Robbie the entire crappy trauma that comes with it. She'll always love Kate and you'll end up coming second place, you watch." She was being a complete bitch and as for slagging Robbie off that was a big fat no in my book.

I picked up the empty glass on the table and poured it full of wine then downed it in one large swig. Looking at her very sternly I said; "Up until I met Robbie I was a complete bitch just like you. So if you want to play mind games, you've just met the best player you could ever find. Now are you going to cut the crap and get over yourself, and give me some insight to what happened in the past between you two?"

"Wow you're kind of ballsy."She replied looking quite impressed. "I'll give you that. Tell you what; I can see you're squeezed for time right now so how about you give me your number and we can arrange a time to meet up."

As she stubbed her cigarette out with her shoe, she leant forward to get closer to me and whispered. "I like you; I like you a lot Sarah Niles. You're my kind of girl."

As I went to get up I could hear Robbie beckoning me. She seemed quite displeased in her tone as she called out that we were leaving. But something was annoying me and I wasn't quite sure what it was but one thing I had noticed; how did Jen know my last name?

"Sarah it's time to go." Robbie snapped as she walked up to us. "I hope Jen hasn't fed you too much poison with her lies. Jen I can't say it's been a pleasure, because it never is with you!" She took me by the hand and led me off back to the house in order to say my goodbye to Kate.

I dropped the piece of paper that I had jotted my number down on, and as we left I looked at Jen who winked at me and made the comment; "Be seeing you real soon Lady Sarah."

My departure from Kate's house was pretty swift as Robbie practically frog marched me out into the street. I could see that she was full of anger, and as we spent the entire walk home in silence her pace became faster, and it was difficult for me to keep up with her. My high heels were definitely no match compared to her boots, and the soles of my feet became sore and gave me cause to limp, but there was no sympathy coming my way. I just wanted to cry the entire way home but my pride wouldn't allow me.

When we reached home her mood had only intensified. She grabbed a beer for herself and then slammed the fridge door shut as if to say, you can get your own! I began to feel a nervousness building

Chapter Six: Bitter Sweet Encounters

inside me as I waited for her emotions to explode. This was new territory to me and I wasn't sure how I was going to react to her outrage.

"How could you lie to me like that, especially in front of Kate?" She snapped at me not caring that I was completely at a loss for words as I had no idea what I was up against. "And to speak to that little tramp, what was it you wanted to know Sarah; did she give you all the details about us? Were my actions towards her not clear enough for you to understand that she's bad news?" When she opened the can of beer she must have shaken it a little because the foam sprayed out and soaked her arm, I found it funny but there was no way that I was going to let her see that.

"Robbie I'm so sorry whatever it is that I've done to upset you I'm really sorry." I pleaded with her intensely. "She didn't tell me anything, it wasn't like that. Why are you so angry with me?"

"Sarah." She said in a firm authoritative voice. "I should never have let my guard down with you. Since meeting you my head has been in complete turmoil over whether I should get involved with you or not. But I saw how much softer your personality had become, compared to when we first met, and I began to trust you. And trust has been the biggest challenge I've had with people. I'm still not sure if I can fully trust you; there is so much we can learn from each other in this relationship, but I don't think it's a good idea that we start with small lies, as they just lead onto bigger lies. And this marriage was already started with one big lie." How could she say all of this wasn't she the cause of this lie in the first place? Double standards were certainly coming to light.

I was so stunned at this point that I was lost for what to say to her. How could I defend myself when I knew she was right, so I thought actions speak louder than words, I'll put my arms around her. But her anger was still fierce and she was certainly not interested in making it any easier for me. Then she informed me that she had some errands to run for Kate and that she would be gone for a couple of hours. The real reason I suspected, was that she wanted to get away from me. Well maybe I needed a little space from her too.

She had been gone for about an hour when I received a text message. It was from Jen. She wanted me to meet her in ten minutes, at the coffee shop just around the corner from my place. Good choice I thought, they make great coffee there. But if I go it means I'm going against Robbie's wishes. No, I just couldn't do it; I'll text her back and tell her I'm not interested. As I finished my message it actually read; I'll be there in five. I stared at it for a moment and wondered if I should send it. My thumb was hovering over the send key whilst my head argued with my heart over what to do. Down I pressed. The need to know about Robbie's past had won the battle for my inquisitive little mind. Although I would have to tell her where I'd gone to when she gets back from Kate's. Hopefully she would see it as, me telling the truth, no more lies for sure.

Walking into the coffee shop I saw that Jen was already sitting at a table by the largest window they had. I told her that her timing was good as Robbie had gone to do some errands for Kate. But somehow Jen already knew that she was. She told me that she made it her business to know everything that was going on with people she had a shared interest in. She even knew of one of my one night stands through a mutual friend. That person turned out to be Debbie. That's when the penny dropped and I realised she had found out information about me before I'd even married Robbie. I felt intimidated but also fascinated by this little trouble maker. She was so quick to come forward with information and told me that she and Robbie had had a yearlong love affair straight after Kate dumped her. She gave Robbie a good time in bed and that the sex was more than just fucking. I hated hearing this and jealousy started to rear its ugly head and fester in the pit of my stomach. It was sex with no morals and that Robbie would allow her to perform sadistic acts during their sessions. As far as she knew, Robbie was in to it for self punishment. It was probably a guilty conscience for not being with Kate. And as far as she knew, Kate didn't have a clue about their antics. Not at the time of their affair anyhow. But she suspected that Robbie has come clean to Kate since. Robbie had always assumed that she and Kate would get married one day, and went into a deep depression when their relationship ended, so Jen became her escape from reality; that Kate might die.

I asked her why Robbie had shown so much hatred towards her and she told me that she had constantly phoned Robbie begging her to stay with her. She followed her around so much that she could have been classed as a stalker. She also came to the conclusion that if she couldn't have Robbie that she would have the next best thing; Robbie's exes. She sought them out one by one and waited until she had gained their confidence and then she shagged them. She claimed that she was not a perfect person in fact far from it but she didn't regret any of it.

I was feeling a little envious and hurt by all of this information when I noticed Jens attentions were slightly focused on the window behind me. Then out of the blue she placed her hands on top of mine, giving them a tight squeeze so that I couldn't escape too quickly. In doing so, a figure stopped in front of the window and I saw it was Robbie standing there staring at us both. She had a look of hurt and despair on her face and it must have looked like there was something going on between us, seeing us so cozy and friendly together. I quickly pulled my hands away from Jens clutches, but it was too late. Robbie had stormed off into the direction of our home. I looked at Jen with dismay and her reaction made me realise that I had just played right into her stinking sadistic game. She may have just ruined the best thing that had ever happened to me; how I kept myself from slapping her I'll never know. I grabbed my bag and coat and ran as fast as I could to catch up to Robbie. It's not easy to do that in high heels, my mind was full of regret and thoughts of how I was going to explain myself to her and as I turned the corner I ran straight into a bicycle that had been left propped up against a wall. There was no chance for me to avoid it and I went flying arse over tit and as I landed one of the stilettos snapped off of my favourite shoes which I classed more important than the black eye that was going to appear in the next few minutes. It had all been too much; the entire second half of the day had turned into a complete shit fest. Even for a drama queen like me; I wasn't aware that lesbian drama was quite so intense. But Jen knew and she also knew that Robbie would be walking past when she did and used it to her advantage to play another round in her vicious spiteful game.

My emotions were high and I was frightened that this sweet woman was going to leave me. She had taken my mind and my heart and turned me into a soppy love sick wreck; a far cry from the stuck up cow I used to be. As I stumbled into the apartment I cried out; "Robbie! Robbie! Where are you? Please believe me it wasn't what it looked like there's nothing going on with her. I'm in love with you; it's you that I want." I had finally said those magical words and for the first time in my life I felt comfortable in saying them even though they were said under rather insane circumstances.

I found her packing her belongings into a case, one of mine of course and in a rather hurried manner too. She was hurt and angry and not ready to listen to any of my shit.

"I'm leaving you Sarah." She spurned as she just shoved everything in without a care. "It's all been about what you want, about your experience. You have deceived me with the one person that has taken the greatest pleasure in hurting me. She is a crazy bitch and made my life a living hell; you have no idea what a nightmare she is. Well you can have her; thanks for breaking my heart Sarah Niles I should never have trusted you."

"But Robbie, I have not deceived you, I just agreed to meet her for a coffee and…"

She rudely interrupted me as she hoisted the bag off the bed. "Oh save it for someone who cares; you went behind my back and that's unforgiveable, we should have never complicated things and I only have myself to blame for that mistake. I'll be in touch soon; you can call off the immigration if you want, I'll find another way to stay if I have to." She was allowing a stupid mix up to cloud her judgement and I just had to make her see sense.

"Robbie I love you doesn't that mean anything to you?" I de-

Chapter Six: Bitter Sweet Encounters

clared my heart and soul to her as my eyes filled up with tears and the onset of panic thrashed at my spirit.

"It's not enough Sarah. Damn it, it's not enough!" There was a momentary pause between us; she had spoken her final words to me and now I was worthless to her.

At that moment she was gone. I was devastated and alone, and for the first time in my life I was choked up at the idea of losing someone; a person that I had let into my heart.

The afternoon turned into evening and my heart began to ache. She wasn't coming back to me! The silence was too much to bear and I cried well into the night;: was this hurt going to last for an eternity.

As morning broke, I could hear the birds singing and the sun was shining through the window so brightly, but none of that mattered to me; all I could think about was how Robbie smiled and laughed, and how she made me feel warm and fuzzy when she wrapped her arms around me and how I felt lonely without her. The whole separation had made me feel sick and I wished for her to forgive me and run back into my arms, but she wasn't intent on returning: not for my sake anyway.

My eyes were swollen and red from the tears and there was no way I could even face going into work. Because I couldn't bring myself to talk to anyone I sent an email to one of the girls who worked there asking her if she could cover for me, just for a few days. But the days I took off turned into a week. Jessica had left several messages on my phone and I knew she was getting worried that I hadn't called her back. She had no idea that I was broken emotionally. I didn't bother to open the curtains the whole time, and the couch became my base. I would get up and go as far as my bedroom door and then because I couldn't face going inside to dwell on the wonderful events that had taken place there, I quit the idea of changing my clothes, and returned back to the couch once again. My hair had become a tangled and wiry mess and dark circles appeared under my eyes from lack of sleep. I was so hungry, but I couldn't face eating a thing. There were bananas left sitting in a bowl on the side table; Robbie had bought them to make smoothies with and they had begun to turn black and the smell was becoming overwhelming but I just couldn't be arsed to deal with them. Letters had been delivered and were piling up at the foot of the door but I couldn't be bothered to get up and open them. Nothing else mattered to me at that point, I felt like I just wanted to die.

As I lay in a crumpled heap on the floor I heard a key turn in the lock and the front door started to open, looking up in hope that Robbie was returning to me my heart quickly sank when I saw it was both my parents standing there.

"Oh Sarah: my poor little sweetheart!" My mother called out and came running over. "What's going on? What's happened to you? Should I call a doctor? Are you in pain? Talk to me sweetheart."

"Oh no mum I'm ok." I said wearily as tried to pull myself together just for appearances sake, Please don't ask so many questions I need to be left alone. I'm alright honest. I really don't need to be fussed over right now." I placed one of the cushions that I had pulled off back onto the couch and tears had left stain marks on one side of it.

"I'm afraid that's exactly why we're here my girl." My father announced looking at me rather seriously.

"We love you very much darling." My mother said holding me like I was a small child. "And when Jessica called us because she was worried about you, we headed straight here." My mother: Pure and perfect how could she understand my torment how could I tell her that I'd broken the law for a total stranger and then fallen in love with her.

"I can see you're not well my angel." My father said as he stroked my hair slowly giving me the assurance that I was still his little princess. "So I'm going to leave your mother here with you just until you're back on your feet again."

"Oh mum, I'm so lost." I sobbed.

"Do you want to talk about it?" She asked in a soft caring motherly tone. "Sarah dear have you gone and got yourself pregnant, is that what this is all about?"

"No mum I'm not. I really can't talk to you about it, you wouldn't understand anyway." I cried.

Chapter Six: Bitter Sweet Encounters

At that she went into the kitchen and made me a sandwich filled with eggs and salad cream. It was one of my favourites when I was growing up at home. She always knew what to feed me when I was down. She sat and watched me take small tiny nibbles, and as I ate more, the nibbles turned into larger bites until it was all gone. Once she was satisfied on seeing an improvement in me, she prompted my father to leave us alone. He gave me a large kiss on my forehead and informed me that he would see me soon and that he loved me very much. After he left, my mother made a start on the cleaning; the place had become rather musty through lack of ventilation. My nostrils were being filled with delightful clean smells of lemon and lavender, and once she opened the curtains and windows for fresh air I felt like I was her little girl again watching her do what she seemed to love doing, housework!

"You can always come back home Sarah, we'd love to have you I hope you know that." She carried on merrily cleaning and humming as she did so and started to re-arrange all of my possessions.

"I know mum, and thanks but I'll be fine." I was lucky to have such caring parents and to know that if all else failed they would be there for me as my back up plan.

"So is it man trouble? Have you lost your job then? Sarah I'm really worried about you."

"Please don't mum." I mumbled as I fought the tears back. "I've spent an entire week crying and now I'm all out of tears. I really can't tell you why I'm so down."

Knowing that my mother was taking care of me, gave me a feeling of being safe, and I managed to fall asleep on the sofa while she pottered around cleaning up the rest of my mess.

CHAPTER SEVEN

PLEASURABLE TORTURE

*I*t was 9am the next morning when I awoke to the smell of bacon and eggs coming from the kitchen. Upon seeing my home immaculate and sparkly I gave my mother a very welcomed hug and stole a piece of bacon from the plate she had just placed down.

"Well seems like someone's perking up." She said and neatly flipped two eggs onto the plate.

"I love you mum." I carried on hugging her as I peered over her shoulder to watch her perform. "You're the greatest, and the place looks great too."

It was just then that I realised she must have been in my bedroom and done a complete overhaul. Opening the door I saw that everything had been cleaned, the bed sheets that I had shared with Robbie, my dressing gown that had Robbie's scent adorned on it. Every trace of her had been deleted, the evidence of my relationship stripped away in moments. I had unknowingly been denied the opportunity to say good bye to her in my own private way. There was however, one of Robbie's tops still hanging in the closet, she called it her beater top and I loved the way it showed off her muscles at the top of her arms. Just as I slipped it on over the top that I was wearing, my mother walked in and commented that it wasn't like me to wear that type of clothing. I smiled politely and looked away so that she wouldn't see me well up.

"Come and eat now darling." She beckoned; "Your breakfast is getting cold."

My appetite had returned rather quickly and I ate everything up on my plate. After eating I made the effort to take a shower, and seeing myself naked in the mirror made me see just how awful I looked. I'd lost weight, my facial features looked drawn in and my eyes had lost their vibrant sparkle causing them to appear lifeless and filled with emotional pain.

Standing under the massaging droplets of water, I began to feel more refreshed and alive again with the fresh scent of citrus lather cleansing away all of my impurities. It gave me wisdom to get the old me back; so I dried myself off, put on some makeup and showed my mother that the daughter she knew and loved was back on track again.

"Mum I feel so much better now." I told her. "I wasn't I'll, I just need you to know that. I had a problem and I didn't know how to deal with it, but I'm over it now. And I think you should be home with dad not with me. He needs you more than I do."

We spent the rest of the day together, catching up on lots of girlie gossip and eating out at a nice restaurant. Then taking a tourists walk through the streets of London, taking in the history of the old buildings and making up stories of what went on inside them all those years ago. By early evening my father had arrived to pick my mother up. We spent the next couple of hours together bringing up all the usual old family memories, before they headed off back to Bristol.

After waving them off I noticed there was a missed call on my mobile and saw that it was Jen so I text her back asking what did she want? She replied; you! This made me nervous and uneasy, what was I supposed to say to that? I replied back that I wasn't available. Several minutes later she replied; that's not what I've heard. I was just about to send her another text back when there was a knock at the door. Upon opening it I was greeted with; "Well are you going to invite me in?"

It was her! She'd made her way over whilst we were texting each other. She was dressed in an extremely short PVC skirt and black stockings shown off by knee high shiny leather boots and a black lacy bra with a red trim and all of this was beneath a long leather coat that made her look excitingly wicked.

"Hello gorgeous." She said seductively and looked me up and down as tho she was ready to devour my body.

"What are you doing here?" I asked totally taken by surprise.

"Let's just say that I've come to entertain you." Her eyes were lustful and full of dare.

She invited herself in and before I could stop her, she grabbed me by the neck and gave me a full kiss on the lips. I was slightly taken back with the gesture but the thing is without understanding why, I kind of enjoyed it. She shut the door with a light force and then removed her coat to reveal her tiny body, with not an ounce of fat anywhere. I couldn't resist touching her slender figure knowing that this was gonna get dirty. She had enslaved me with her power of seduction and I found my hands travelling aimlessly up and down her back as I lead her into the bedroom still interlocked in a kiss. She gained total charge of the situation and pushed me down onto the bed then removed my clothing in a rather savage manner and whilst literally ripping my knickers off, she commanded me to; shut the fuck up and do as I'm told. Her dominance was a big turn on, one moment she would be gentle with me giving a false sense of security then without warning a light slap on the butt followed by pinching on the nipples or biting my body just hard enough for it to hurt. She was forceful as she used her fingers inside me, but it was like a good pain, something I wanted more of as she put my body through pleasurable sexual torture. I never thought that this was a possibility. When she was finished with me there were no words spoken between us. She held a self satisfied look on her face, and whilst leaving me on the bed naked and feeling used she got up and just left, without even looking back. I felt strange and unsure of what had just occurred and pulled the sheets up around my shamed naked body. She was a sexy babe with a hot look but I didn't feel fulfilled from this experience, maybe that's because she wasn't Robbie.

I needed to talk to someone and Jessica was my best friend the only one who understood me. I called her up and we arranged to meet in our local pub, so I revamped my makeup and tidied up my hair before making my way to join her.

As I greeted her the first thing she asked me was; why was I acting so strangely? I couldn't blurt out that I'd been had by a sex kitten: I was unsure of how she would react to knowing that I'd just had lip-

Chapter Seven: Pleasurable Torture

stick sex with a practical stranger and for now I just wanted to concentrate on Robbie and how I was going to exist without her.

We hugged each other and ordered our drinks whilst filling in the gaps of the past week. She acknowledged and understood the mental suffering that I was going through, and made statements of all my good points toasting to each one of them to make me feel better. She also informed me that she had been seeing Jake, on several occasions, and that a relationship had been forming between them. I was pleased that she was comfortable enough to talk about him with me and as the night went on we got so drunk that our words were becoming slurred and I couldn't stop myself from singing out loud to every song that played on the duke box. I ended up staying the night at her place and we carried on our drinking session well into the early hours.

The hangover I woke up with lasted until late that afternoon, but even with that, I'm glad we partied.

Over the next few weeks I kept myself busy; joining a gym was a great idea, and I had gained definition in my arms due to all the working out that I was doing, and I had the best looking butt I'd ever seen. I also put more hours into my job, making sure each customer left the store spending more than they had intended to, and I even made some rather large bonuses out of it too.

I had a pleasant surprise one morning when Kate walked in to the store. She looked fantastic, her hair had grown a little and had a delicate shine to it, and her figure was getting back into shape; actually her entire presence was glowing.

"Hi." I said as I kissed her on the cheek. "So what brings you here today I mean it's good to see you. How are you? You look amazing Kate."

"Oh I'm doing fine." She replied smiling sweetly. "I'm gaining strength every day and I've actually come out shopping with a friend today. I think you remember her; Jen."

From the way that Kate spoke, it sounded as though she wasn't aware of what had occurred and that maybe Robbie hadn't told her about my earlier encounter with Jen.

"How is Robbie?" I bravely asked her. My eyes were fixated towards the window so that she couldn't see the hurt in them and I fiddled around with a rack of dresses that were hanging on wooden hangers, pretending I was quite busy with them.

She put her hand on my arm as if to comfort me and said; "I think she's fine. I'm not exactly sure what happened between you two; she hasn't spoken too much about it. I've tried to talk to her, but all she says is that it's over between you. I'm sorry Sarah; I thought you two were so well matched. I just don't get it."

"That's ok Kate." I answered with a loud sigh. "My life seems to have a way of turning to shit lately so maybe that's my destiny."

As I showed her some items she might be interested in I got a glimpse of Jen walking towards us. She had a smug look on her face, as if she enjoyed playing games with people's lives; especially mine, and all I could do was cringe as she spoke with such arrogant confidence.

"Hello there Sarah Niles and how's that pretty cute arse of yours, still feeling the pain are we? Wow you're looking pretty hot there girl have you been working out?" This woman was insane if she thought she could get away with making comments out in the open like that.

I felt myself go red with embarrassment. Was she going to say something to Kate about what we had done? I did not need reminding of this encounter and certainly did not want my personal life on display. God what a fool I've been.

As Kate went to try on a few items in the changing room Jen made a comment to ridicule me; "Did you enjoy our little liaison lover girl?"

"Look!" I said trying to keep my voice in a low tone. "It was a one off, I wasn't thinking straight and I think you caught me at a bad time in my life and I just want to forget about it. Please just leave it where it belongs, in the past!"

"Hey lover girl I think you need to hear something." She whispered into my ear. "You allowed me to fuck you and I know you'll never forget me." Her hand had miraculously found its way to my

Chapter Seven: Pleasurable Torture

ass, squeezing it playfully but I was quick to reject her advance and removed it; digging my nails into her skin as I did so.

"Just get the hell away from me I'm not interested in what you've got to say. You're sick and twisted in your head."

Shoving her out of my personal space I went and picked out a few more items for Kate to try on and waited by her door in hope that Jen would shut her big fat mouth. Oh god was I wrong; she followed me in and spoke loud enough for Kate to hear everything that she had to say.

"So working out really suits you, you look a lot fitter than when I last saw you. I'm turned on girl, how about going for a second round? The first one was just to tease you."

I knew Kate had heard everything, and with her knowing Jen as well as she did, I'm sure she knew what she meant. As Kate came out of the changing room her face was red.

She handed me the items that she wanted to purchase, and whilst paying for them she went a little cold on me. She had understood what happened between us and I felt crushed and ashamed. Had I unwittingly just gained a new enemy?

Before she left, she pulled me aside and said in a quiet voice; "I've seen that look before Sarah. I saw it in Robbie's eyes just after we broke up. I knew what she had been up to with Jen. She punished herself in guilt of my illness by letting Jen torture her and she blamed herself for not taking better care of me. But to be honest my condition was not down to her." It was obvious to me why Robbie had been so in love with Kate and I began to appreciate greatly the relationship that they once had.

'Thank you Kate." I said shamefully. "I really appreciate your concern and please feel free to call in any time."

"Please keep in touch Sarah. I see a good friend in you and I'll tell Robbie that I saw you. Bye for now." She was genuinely sincere and I felt that we had just grown a little closer.

"Goodbye Kate." I called out after her as she exited the doorway. "And it's good to see you looking so healthy!"

She was followed closely by Jen who annoyingly managed to whisper behind Kate's back; "Bye lover girl, see you soon." And then she cheekily blew me a kiss.

I felt awkward and if Jen ever let on to Robbie what had occurred between us I would surely die. Why had I allowed myself to get into this situation?

It was time to close the store for the evening and after sending everyone home I stayed behind to take care of restocking some of the items and tidying up a little. Suddenly I was startled when I caught a glimpse of movement coming from behind a row of long dresses that were now looking rather dishevelled so I cautiously walked over to see what it could possibly be and parted the garments slowly, I stood silent for a short moment and listened for any sound to come but there was nothing so just as I peered in through a gap expecting to see a mouse or something small and ridiculous but I was only to be faced by the ever loving Jen. She had crept back into the store and hidden out of sight until everyone had left. She was holding a bottle of wine and two glasses and making a gesture of offering me a drink by holding them out towards me.

"Hi there lover girl, why don't you come and join me for a drink, just as a friendly gesture I won't bite you." She said with a snake like tone, vying to secure my trust.

"No Jen I can't, I really need you to leave now. Please just go you're not welcome here."

"I don't give a shit if I'm not welcome." She stated as she twisted the top off the bottle. "I'm not here to form a relationship with you. Just humour me and share some of this good wine. I'm sure you'll like it." She was very persistent and sure of herself and it seemed as though she had no intensions of leaving without having a bitch showdown first.

"Ok just a small glass and that's it." I said, anxious about her motive. "If I have one will you leave straight after?"

"Maybe I will." She said as she poured a full glass out and offered it to me.

Chapter Seven: Pleasurable Torture

I downed my drink as fast as I could, hoping that she would soon leave.

"Now come on lover that was too fast, I'd say you were trying to cheat, here have another." She urged, then grabbed my hand and pulled it towards her filling my glass to the brim. Before long the bottle had been emptied and I started to get a little merry.

"That's my girl." She said in an encouraging manner. "It's a good job I have a second bottle in my bag isn't it, you greedy thing."

She suggested walking me home, and to be honest I was at the point where I needed the help. That was the last thing I remembered as I completely blacked out.

Waking up the next morning my head hurt like hell, and I could hardly move. One of my wrists had been handcuffed to the bed side table and I yanked at it to try to break free.

"What's going on?" I asked as I tried to regain what little I could remember.

A soft voice spoke, and as I turned over I saw Jen lying next to me. "You really like to be bitten, don't you sexy?"

I looked down and saw bite marks all over my breasts and stomach, and I felt sore between my legs. I saw that she was wearing a black leather harness and a rather large silicone penis was protruding out from it and then I understood why I felt so raw inside.

"We were at it for hours my little hoar." She was so proud to announce.

The humiliation was all too much. I couldn't believe this had happened to me, not like this. As she undid my cuffs, I jumped out of the bed as fast as I could; pulling a sheet off with me so I could cover my naked state. The room was spinning around me as I tried to focus and steadied myself against the wall for support.

"Oh come on, it was just a bit of fun, that's all. I don't see why you suddenly have a problem now." She sneered and teased me by tugging at the sheet but I was having none of it.

"You fucking bitch! You fucked me with that huge thing for hours. I feel like my insides have been ripped apart. Get out! Just fucking get out Jen. Robbie was right you are a crazy sadistic bitch." I picked up a pillow and threw it at her face; not that it had any impact but I felt good for doing it.

"Oh sweetheart how you wanted me last night, you enjoyed everything I did to you. Don't be so hostile, you're the one who asked me to bite you and slap you and get a little rough. You've got hostility shoved right up your ass; you're just a cock tease."

As she dressed to leave, she informed me that Robbie would be interested to know that I had enjoyed the same pleasurable experience that she had. And that I was even hotter and fitter than the first time we shagged. There was nothing that I could do to stop her. She had the upper hand on me, but I called her bluff anyway and told her to go ahead and tell Robbie, as our relationship had come to an abrupt end before it had been given a chance to even get started.

When she left it took a while for me to calm down and after drinking the hair of the dog I tended to the scratches and bite marks that bitch had so generously given me. Then searching my closet for something to wear that would hide the reminders I came across Robbie's top again and made the decision to wear it. It made me look a little tomboyish in a pretty hot way and I matched it with a pair of tight fitting jeans and tied my hair back in a pony tail. I wanted to know what it would feel like to live the same kind of life as Robbie, to walk in her shoes and be a part of her world exploring the fascinating lesbian fun ride. So far my introduction to this life had had its faults but the need to continue over ruled the need not to.

CHAPTER EIGHT
WHEN LIES BECOME THE TRUTH

That night I went to the Pink Rainbow club by myself. It was full of women having a good time so I sat at a table in a corner and watched the activities going on around me whilst drinking a pint of beer. It felt strange to be more on the masculine side rather than my usual girlie self, and I could see that I was being eyed up by more than one dyke, so maybe showing off my pecks really was the way to get noticed.

One woman came over and introduced herself as Chloe, she would never be the type I'd consider hunting but she did have a nice look about her and I felt comfortable when we were talking. She had green eyes and long mousey brown hair that covered her broad shoulders and she constantly kept flicking her curls with her hands. It was annoying and frustrating to not be able to tell her how that was a turn off.

"Have you been working out?" She asked and gave my arm a quick squeeze. "I do love a fit woman."

"Yeah so many people are noticing." I said in a cool fashion; flattery was a good way for her to secure a small portion of my attention.

I didn't give her too much information about myself; I just listened to the chat up crap she had to offer and while she was going on about her past girlfriends and to be honest did I really give a shit; my thoughts turned to Robbie and how this girl held no comparison to her. The only way I could get the woman I loved out of my mind was to get laid by as many girls as I could, and start having a good time; I had to shut this dyke up she was driving me insane with her boring useless information so I got straight to the point; "So do you want to fuck now or later?" Pretty straight to the point I thought.

She replied; "Wow you're not shy, are you? The answer is yes, I want to fuck you now."

"Then take me back to yours so we can get down to business." I'd already forgotten her name, but that didn't matter too much as she was so busy planting her wet sloppy lips on to mine as we sat in the back seat of the cab.

Her place was small and dingy and she obviously didn't have too much money to spare on decent furniture. I had no intentions of making her feel good so I just went through the motions of what was needed to be done. The sex was unemotional and it felt like I had a duty to carry on to the end. I stayed for a few hours and then left while she was still sleeping. As soon as I got home, I immediately jumped into the shower and cleansed off the guilt that I felt dirty and disgusted with myself, something I had never found to be in my former non caring days.

One night stands used to be ok for me, but since meeting Robbie my whole outlook on life has changed. For a start I was actually beginning to have morals, well sort of if you don't count last night or my liaison with Jen; twice! And my personality had become much softer, which that fact is true, but all the time I wanted what I had just lost. Being told that time is a great healer didn't work for me, my feelings for Robbie only got stronger each day, and I was now at the point in my head and my heart that I wanted to say the words, I love you to her, and for her to reciprocate them back to me.

The following morning the post arrived and in with it was an invitation to a wedding. It was from Jessica. She and Jake had decided on a date, rather quickly I thought, but then who was I to be a judge on the love tracker. I called her immediately to congratulate her, although I did have my nagging suspicions about their relationship and whether it was for real, I never let on. She asked me to be her maid of honour and I squealed as I accepted the offer. We spoke for ages, and I was finally able to pour my heart out to her about my female conquests, and the humiliation that I had recently gone through. She was good at keeping my secret confessions that I had made, and I felt kind of relieved to have shared them with her.

The weeks went by and the morning of Jessica's wedding had

Chapter Eight: When Lies Become the Truth

arrived. I could see the excitement in her eyes; she was glowing and looked so beautiful in her fairytale gown that had been adorned with crystals and beads and the long veil finished off the look quite romantically.

"I love him Sarah." She said as she picked up her bouquet of lilac and white flowers. "Now put your dress on before I get all tearful."

I put on my lilac strapless dress that she had bought me, and these cute little silver heels. My hair was pinned up on top of my head with tiny wispy bits cascading down and caressing my cheeks and small white flowers complimented the look.

Our ride to the church was in a white Rolls Royce, and didn't we feel special. Jessica's dress took up most of the room of course and I had to keep patting it down every time she moved. We just kept looking at each other and laughing. Comments about my wedding day were flowing; literally at my expense, and it all seemed quite funny now.

During the service; actually Jessica was just about to say I do, I received a text message. My phone didn't have one of the quietists ring tones and I got a lot of disapproving looks and a few comments from the other guests; shame on them for being more interested in my goings on rather than being focused on the bride and groom.

"Oh my God, it's her." I yelled out without thinking; my voice echoed throughout the church. It was a little embarrassing to say the least.

A man sitting behind me told me to shush. How rude was that! Jessica turned around to see what all the fuss was about.

"It's from Robbie." I mouthed; excited that she was finally contacting me.

She gave me a pleasing smile and then turned back around to carry on with her facade; I mean ceremony. I on the other hand couldn't believe that I was reading a message from Robbie. Finally, finally she wanted to see me. The excitement was all too much and I couldn't contain myself so I rushed outside to reply back to her. Now that was showing consideration to the other guests wasn't it?

Ok tomorrow at Kate's then, I wrote. I gave a momentary pause before sending it, still in awe that the woman I had fallen in love with had contacted me.

This day just couldn't have got any better for me, and wearing a beaming smile for most of it, I found that I had attracted the attentions of one of the male guests. He made it perfectly clear to me what he wanted to do to my hot body, so I flirted with him a little before telling him that I'd bet him fifty quid that I could end up in bed with the dark haired bridesmaid before he did. He took the hint quite well I thought. The word lesbian only spattered from his mouth once.

I chose to drink only one glass of champagne the entire day as I wanted to look refreshed and beautiful for Robbie, and turning up with a hangover was completely out of the question. I was going to look so gorgeous that she would realise that she'd made a huge mistake and would pull me into her arms and never let me go again.

It was 11.30 pm and I really needed to make a move and get home so I thanked Jessica and Jake for such a wonderful day and managed to get a ride with the bridesmaid that I had bet on earlier. As we drove away I saw the look of surprise from the man who had tried to pick me up, so I gave him a really big wink and blew him a kiss.

I had only managed to get a few hours of sleep due to the excitement of seeing Robbie today so I put two slices of cucumber over my eyes to freshen them up and gave myself plenty of time to get ready. I used the most subtle choice of makeup and put on the lightest scent of perfume. I knew that Robbie liked that kind of look on me. Remembering that she liked me in my white button up shirt that showed off my bra, I chose to wear it with a tight pair of black trousers, giving me the look of a professional business woman. I now felt more in control of the situation and the only thing that was left for me to do was to figure out what I was going to say.

I called a cab and a short time later I was standing outside Kate's front door. My heart was beating fast and I found it hard to control my breathing. The palms of my hands were clammy and my nerves kicked in just as I rang the doorbell.

Chapter Eight: When Lies Become the Truth

I could hear footsteps approaching on the other side of the door and I cleared my throat ready for the big speech but as it was opened rather aggressively I received a horrifying shock as I was faced by the one and only vindictive Jen. My heart sank as she glared at me. Could I not get this smug bitch out of my life? She stood elegant and silent with her hands firmly rested on her hips.

"I'm here to see Robbie." I said with a stern voice. "Kindly step aside, I know my way in."

"She's not here." The words she greeted me with snapped out of her mouth instantly and she held no regret when she saw the hurt look on my face. "She's out with Kate and she won't be back for hours, but she did leave these documents for you to sign. That's if you still want to."

She reached at a table behind her and then shoved some papers into my hands, and told me to sign on the highlighted parts. As I looked them over I could see that they were from immigration. It was down to me whether Robbie stayed or not. I hesitated for a moment before signing each page and then handed them back to her quite resentfully. She had probably been privy to my personal information and now knew everything about me.

"Be quick Sarah." She snarled impatiently. "I'm just on my way out to meet a really hot chick. Say if you're not doing anything today I'm sure she wouldn't mind us having a threesome; so how about it lover?" She licked her lips like a salacious hot slut in a porn movie would. She actually made me shudder.

"You really make me sick." I screamed so loud at her that it made my throat hurt and I had to pause momentarily. "Why don't you just crawl into a corner and die."

I quickly turned about with my head held high and walked away with dignity, not letting her see the tears filling up in my eyes. I had foolishly believed that I was going to be reunited with Robbie. That cow Jen must have told her all about our sexual encounters and relished in the pain that she was causing me; just because she could. I know that that information would have hurt Robbie immensely, as

Jen had unwittingly become her nemesis. I had fallen into the web of deceit and now I was paying a hefty fine for it.

I began to cry uncontrollably as I walked down the street and I held my stomach tight as a sickened feeling overwhelmed me. I grabbed my mouth hard so no one could hear my cries of woe. My makeup was streaming down my cheeks and making my eyes sting and my legs were turning to jelly as I felt as though I was just about to collapse.

I hadn't heard Kate's voice calling me from the other side of the street. She had spotted me in my distressed state and tried to get my attention. As she managed to get to me, I fell into her arms with an awful feeling of nothing to live for.

"My sweet Sarah, what's happened?" She said in a comforting way. "Are you ok? Come on let me take you home, we can talk there."

It was the last place I wanted to be but I had no choice. She sat me on the couch and passed me a pack of tissues and a box of fine Belgian chocolates to boost my sugar level and I managed to scoff them in one fowl swoop; but as the chocolate melted in my mouth it dripped down my chin and stained my shirt. Once I had finished sobbing, at least to a more controllable stage, I managed to tell her about my arrangements with Robbie, and how Jen had managed to weave her ugliness into the situation.

"I mean if Robbie didn't want to see me, then why the hell didn't she just post the papers?" I carried on sobbing as I looked at Kate for answers hoping that she had some insight to Robbie's actions.

"But Robbie went to meet you. You sent her a note saying it was of great importance. She must be waiting at the coffee shop now." She informed me as she tried to relocate the note that she had read.

"But Kate I never sent her a note." I replied totally confused and quickly joined her in the search for this mystery piece of paper.

It was then that Kate realised that Jen was at the core of all of this. She had kicked Jen out a couple of days ago. Apparently there was a big argument between them when she informed Kate that she had

Chapter Eight: When Lies Become the Truth

been servicing me the same way she did Robbie, and that Kate wasn't falling for her bullshit anymore. She was also angry that Robbie had fallen for her lies and made Jen leave right at that moment. She must have stolen a set of keys to get back in to the house and deceive me even further with her pretence and sordid mind games.

I took a big gulp of air before I made my confession. "But wait a minute Kate; I have to be honest with you about this. You see she isn't lying about us; she did seduce me, but it was after Robbie left me and I had lost total control of my life. I had hit rock bottom and I wasn't thinking straight. She meant absolutely nothing to me, it just happened!"

That was the wrong time for me to confess my sins; Robbie had been standing in the doorway without us hearing her come in and heard everything that had stupidly flown out of my big fat mouth. She was appalled with the idea of me having any kind of intimacy with Jen, especially as she had given a lot of thought about us and was in the process of making it up with me.

The look of hurt was written all over her face and in a broken voice she said; "You'll never change will you Sarah? Always getting what you want, you're a heart breaker; I can't believe that I doubted Jens lies. Only they weren't lies were they?"

"Robbie I've changed, I'm not what you think I am."

"Oh just save it Sarah." She barked at me. "I don't want to hear anymore of your crap." In the same instance I had won Robbie back and then lost her again, through foolish meaningless sex. She stormed out of the house and down the street and was gone. I was left alone with Kate, who by this time had built up a lot of sympathy for me. Her kindness had overwhelmed me and I wondered why.

She explained that she too had faced matters with Jen in the past. That to this day she wasn't sure of all the details with her and Robbie and that she didn't want to know. It seemed that Jen had set out to destroy all relationships that Robbie encountered and succeeded in doing so and that she has been in love with Robbie, if that's what you want to call it, since she first met her.

She told me that Robbie has been through hell with Jen, the constant phone calls, the stalking, the letters. That it had been going on for some time, but she thought it had actually died down lately as Jen was showing kindness and consideration. I now understood why Robbie was so untrusting; how it was better for her to marry a total stranger; someone who apparently couldn't get hurt, but they did.

I ended up staying for hours, and we ate dinner together as Kate cheered me up. She informed me that Jen had bragged with explicit details of my drunken sex scandal, and I was so ashamed because I'd blacked out I couldn't remember half of it. Poor Robbie having to listen to that, it must have been quite hurtful.

As evening approached I thanked Kate for looking after me and then made my way home.

Jessica had left several messages on my phone, asking how my meeting went with Robbie. When I called her back and explained everything I felt quite selfish to dominate the conversation; my best friend had just spent her first night as a married woman and we were talking about me. I eventually asked her how she was feeling, and she gave a giggle in a shameful manner and said she loved being married to Jake. That he saw to her needs before his own. One up for Jessica; he never gave me the full service; maybe he did have genuine feelings for her after all.

"Was he like that with you?" She asked inquisitively.

"Well umm, this is awkward." I replied, wondering where this conversation was leading.

She told me that it was ok because I had him first. So I let her know that sex with Jake wasn't how it should have been. I never really cared how he got his rocks off because I was too drunk to care, and that I used him just like all the other guys I'd slept with. She commented that she thought I'd probably been a lesbian all my life and that I just hadn't been aware of it until now. Thinking about it, I never did enjoy being touched by a guy and I definitely would never go down on him. Being with Robbie had shown me what I had been missing. And Jen! Well I have no fucking idea.

"What's it like being with a woman?" She asked. "Or should I not be asking you that?"

"Yes you can ask me that." I told her. "It's softer and gentler, and so affectionate each time is like making love for the first time."

"I am worried about you, are you happy with yourself, I mean really happy?" She asked.

"I'm ok, I promise. I just miss the hell out of Robbie that's all, she was my first true love, and I ache for her." My heart was in pieces, but it wasn't right to inflict that on my newly married friend. She was amazed to hear me talking with a softer tone in my heart, and how my attitude towards people and life had changed. She insisted that we go out together that night, which I questioned, as she'd only been married for one day. But she assured me that Jake was the one doing all the insisting.

"I won't take no for an answer." She sang down the phone. "Get your glad rags on babe and be ready for eight o'clock."

Later that evening I could hear Jessica outside yelling from the street, so I went to the balcony to see what she was doing.

"Sarah! Sarah! Say hi to Jake he's just dropped me off." She tugged at his arm while he sat in the car and encouraged him to play along with her.

I leant over the railing and waved down to him and I could see an excited Jessica giving him a big soppy kiss through the car window before he drove off. I shouted out to him; "Thanks Jake I really appreciate this."

She didn't stop waving until he was out of site, and then she looked up at me with big doe eyes, wearing a strapless red dress and holding a bottle of champagne in her hand.

"What's that in aid of?" I shouted down.

"Oh why the hell not let's celebrate everything." She said in excitement. "Now let me in you slutty hag."

We downed the champers as I finished getting ready, and then followed that with a bottle of chardonnay. The land of happy was upon us. As I completed my cool look, Jessica noticed how fit I was looking and gave my muscles a squeeze.

"God Sarah, you've got some pecks there haven't you. I can see that working out really suits you. I'm impressed."

"Thanks." I said as I gave myself a good look over. "I've put a lot of effort into getting my body physically fit. It helps me take my mind off things that I don't want to think about."

"So where are we going?" Jessica asked as she checked through my new wardrobe of clothes. "Can we go somewhere new and exciting?" I knew exactly where I could take her.

"Yes sure, I know a place we can go, finish your drink and I'll get us a cab."

As I'm paying the cab driver Jessica jumps out and the first thing she shouts in her drunken manner is; "Oh my God it's a lezzie club!"

I just shook my head and smiled, as this was a first for her after all.

CHAPTER NINE

THREE UP TWO DOWN

*T*he noise from the music drowned out any conversation that we attempted, so we found ourselves mostly watching girls getting hot and sweaty on the dance floor.

"I can't tell if that one's a girl or a boy." She pointed out.

"Jessica will you stop staring." I told her. "There are no males in here. Now I need to pee and I suppose you want to follow me?"

We ended up sharing the same cubicle, one of our girlie traditions, and half way through mid pee I recognised a voice in the cubicle next to us.

"Shush Jessica I need to hear." I whispered and put my finger to her mouth as if to quieten her and clumsily tried to do my jeans up with one hand in the process.

She kept laughing and I found it difficult to listen. Then it hit me. It was Jen, she was with someone and it sounded like they were getting it on. We could hear lots of kissing and heavy breathing, and bumping around. Jessica's eyes were big with excitement; she couldn't believe she was listening to two girls fucking.

"Oh my God I think she's having an orgasm." She giggled.

"Jessica will you please be quiet?" I whispered. "It's not like you haven't shagged in the toilets before."

We pulled the lock slowly so they wouldn't hear us and as we crept quietly to the sink, their cubicle door opened and just like clockwork Jens mouth started moving and spat out her usual viciousness. "Oh look who it is. My sexy lover girl! Well I didn't think I'd ever see you in here."

I could see that the girl she was with was checking me out as if to say; fuck off bitch she's with me.

I began to touch up my makeup and watched Jen perform her

usual bitchy act in the reflection of the mirror so I showed her that I wasn't bothered and carried on refreshing my lipstick. As I did so she walked up behind me and stroked my hair whilst staring at Jessica.

"So my little hot conquest, who's this you're with?" She questioned with a look of lust on her face.

"Piss off Jen." I shouted. "You've caused more than enough trouble for me."

"Oh touchy, touchy well you soon got over Robbie with this little hottie." She said as she looked Jessica up and down.

I informed her that I wasn't with Jessica in that way and that we'd been best friends for years. She seemed to be turned on by Jessica's looks and asked her where she'd been hiding all this time. Jessica blushed and giggled, then began to play with her hair; this was something she did when she was being chatted up by a guy she liked.

Jen looked at the girl that she had just shagged and made it clear that she was done with her. The girl looked really pissed off that she had just been dismissed and stormed off. I grabbed Jessica's arm and pulled her back to the dance floor. As we carried on moving rhythmically to the music I suggested to Jessica that I'd get us some more drinks. I was only gone for a few moments but apparently that was long enough for Jen to get her claws into her.

Erotic music was playing and Jen began to dance seductively from behind Jessica, making sure that she had a hand on her body at all times. I watched as she made her moves on my friend, getting in closer and tighter as the song went on. Jessica was too drunk to take it all in so I made my way over to her, spilling some of my beer as I bumped into other dancers.

"Jessica come on I've got drinks, let's sit down." I begged her.

"I'll be there in a minute." She said slurring her words. "I'm having fun with, what's your name again?"

She always has been a bit of a tart, not far from my former self, but I was surprised she had been taken in by a woman. After the song finished she came back and joined me, totally breathless and sweat beading down her face.

"Woo! That was fun." She screamed.

"Well I'm glad you're having a good time. Here drink this you look like you need it." I said, pointing to her beer.

She leaned in towards me and commented; "I know you hate her Sarah, I was just having fun and I promise that the rest of the night belongs to you."

We ended up having a good time and got completely wrecked and when it came time to leave Jessica phoned Jake to come and pick us up. When he arrived I sat in the back of the car and we all sang songs that were playing on the radio. Then I saw Jake lean across to Jessica and say; "Did you ask her?"

"Ask me what?" I slurred and slumped over the back of Jessica's seat.

"No Jake I didn't." I heard her say. "But I got some else's number who'd be interested."

"Hey ask me what?" I repeated, feeling as though I was invisible to them both.

"It's ok Sarah, we've sorted it." Jake announced.

At that point I passed out on the back seat and Jake had to carry me upstairs to my apartment and put me into bed. As I stirred I put my arms around his neck and said; "I love you guys, if Jessica loves you then I do too."

My night was completed and I didn't wake until the next afternoon. My mouth was dry and my head was swimming. It was a major task getting to the bathroom to take a pee and then make my way to the sofa. I lay there for a few more hours before I felt well enough to get up again.

I was beginning to feel hungry but couldn't face cooking anything so I popped round to the coffee shop and ordered a bagel to go with my extra large coffee. Upon enjoying my breakfast and reading a magazine that someone had left behind, I looked up to see that Jen was standing at the counter.

I crouched down as low as I could and hid behind the magazine as best as I could.

"Is that for your sex change op?" She shouted out and pointed at me.

The front cover had an article about male enhancement on it and I could see that she relished in embarrassing me. I could have just slapped her, so I tried to ignore her when she came over and bragged about getting Jessica's phone number and that she had arranged a threesome with her and Jake. I was horrified at this news, because Jessica knew how I felt about this piece of trash. What the hell was she thinking? But then who was I to judge? I hadn't lived an innocent life myself, so how could I tell a grown woman what to do!

"Get lost Jen, I have nothing else to say to you!" I muttered under my breath so no one could hear me.

"I just thought I'd let you know, lover, that I don't go away that easily." She said as she revelled in her glory. "I'm gonna make you sorry that you ever laid your pretty little eyes on Robbie."

Cold chills were running down my body as the thought of her in my life made me feel physically sick. I quickly got up out of my seat and brushed past her as I exited the shop and hastily made my way down the street constantly looking behind to see that she hadn't followed me. I vigorously searched my pockets for my phone, so that I could talk to Jessica and advise her on the trouble that she was going to encounter.

When I urged her not to go through with it, she explained to me, that she and Jake had been talking about it for a while and that they were actually going to ask me to join them, but Jen got in there first. I couldn't believe what I was hearing. How in this short space of time had she become as fucked up as I had?

"Are you insane? Do you know what you are getting into?" I shouted, as I held the phone out in temper.

"Sarah its ok babe this isn't the first time that we've have carried out our sexual fantasies. You are not the only one who has kept secrets locked away. Honestly this isn't new to me." she protested invidiously.

My mind was unsettled, as I knew Jessica was in for a rollercoaster ride with this cow. It wasn't the thought of her having a threesome; it was the thought of her having it with Jen that got me and the knowledge that Jen will have a hold on them for as long as she feels like it will most certainly destroy their relationship.

I found myself walking towards their place, hoping to find that they'd been at the magic chocolate brownies and that this was just a load of crap that they were talking. I just couldn't leave it and I just had to talk sense into both of them.

When I got there, Jessica answered the door and seemed rather flustered. She was quite surprised that it was me standing there and reading the expression on her face I could tell she was expecting Jen.

As we all sat down together I pleaded with them both not to go through with it, but all I got from them was that their personal life was their own business. I couldn't deny that and during my unheard plea the door bell rang and Jessica jumped up rather awkwardly.

"Maybe this isn't a good time to be discussing this right now." She hinted to Jake.

I knew that it was Jen at the door, the sex they were about to have with her had dominated the whole situation and there was nothing that I could do to stop them.

When I left; ignoring Jen's unpleasant remarks as I passed her, I made my way to the Pink Rainbow and downed a couple of pints of beer quite quickly in frustration. Images of the three of them at it kept flashing through my mind so I held my glass up and made a toast to myself, cheering to all the fuck ups that had happened to me lately.

The club started to get busy and the dance floor became full of energetic females all out having a good time. The vibration of the music was rippling through my body so I got up and danced to a few numbers and mingled with the crowd freely.

A woman with olive skin and a strong masculine look made her way over to me, and with a bottle of beer in one hand, and may I say, drinking it in rather a sexy way, she put the other hand around my waist and gently rocked with me.

"My name's Sarah." I shouted over the sound of the loud music.
"Shush, just enjoy." That was her introduction.

I ran my fingers up and down her arms feeling her mighty strength and gazed directly into her eyes waiting for her to make her move. She gave me a feeling of warmth as I snuggled in closer to her body.

Her similarity to Robbie was uncanny and the thought of; I want to keep this one, ran through my mind.

She gently took me by my hand and led me to the washrooms, where we found an unoccupied cubicle and began to make out. As we progressed from light kissing to a more raunchy passionate attack of the lips, she pushed me up against the wall with her powerful arms and nibbled at my top, pulling it away from my breasts and then letting it go, allowing it to smack them back hard. No words were said between us, but I knew I wanted her then and there. I undid my top to reveal my bra to her, my eyes fixated on hers all the time. She nodded her head in an upward direction as if summoning me to take it all off and it took me just seconds to remove my attire. I had become so horny, and as she used her tongue all over my breasts she lifted me up and sat me on the mounted toilet roll holder allowing me to wrap my legs around her waist permitting her to do with me as she wished.

I could feel her fondling the belt on her jeans, and once undone she pushed my knickers to one side, watching my face constantly. She was wearing a strap on in a harness and as she entered me with it, I grabbed her tightly as she pushed me up and down using the wall as my support. My pleasure showed and I told her to fuck me harder and faster. I wanted the pain of sexual excitement as I could feel myself building up ready to orgasm closer and closer. Then as I released myself on her, she slowed her pace down to a more controlled tender act. But she wasn't finished with me yet. She lowered me down slowly, steadying me as she did so and then went down on her knees. She certainly knew how to use her tongue on a woman and within a few minutes I was once again building up into a frenzied orgasm exploding inside me, causing my legs to become a little shaky as I felt spent.

Chapter Nine: Three Up Two Down

Once the act was completed, she stood up and I pulled my skirt back down and put my top back on, and she introduced herself as Charlie.

"My real name is Charlotte, but my image doesn't really go with that so my friends shortened it." She seemed extremely laid back and quite sure of herself but she knew how to control a situation.

As I brushed my hair back, still in awe at what had just taken place, I again informed her that my name is Sarah.

"C'mon Sarah I'll buy you a drink." She offered in a pleasing way, as though she had just won a prize. "Are you ok to walk? You seem a bit off balance."

"I'm alright thank you." I said politely as the inside of my body was still enjoying the after effects.

We sat at a table joining her friends and by the way they reacted, they completely understood what had just taken place.

"This is Kez, this is Jules, guys this is Sarah." She introduced us as she picked up two bottles and passed me one of them.

They nodded their heads up and down at the same time as if in agreement on their approval.

I sat on Charlie's lap just like a trophy wife and she stroked my legs up and down constantly as we chatted away. They seemed like a friendly bunch and it made a refreshing change not to hear any bitching. As I was getting sleepy from the lateness and the alcohol intake I nuzzled my head into Charlie's shoulder and began to drift off.

"Do you want me to take you home babe?" She offered in a sweet concerned manner.

"Yes please, that would be really nice." I whispered into her ear.

She put her arms around me, giving a little squeeze as she informed me that I was safe now. It was as though she knew about my depression and my neediness to be wanted and loved by someone who would protect me.

She took me back to her place, one that she shared with Kez and Jules, and as we climbed into bed together I broke down into tears, and had to tell her how I felt about Robbie and not knowing how to move on from her. She was impressed by my honesty and held me all night as we lay there, not letting me go once.

I awoke to the aroma of coffee brewing and could hear female voices happily chatting away downstairs. I was a little dazed and wasn't too sure of where I actually was. My clothes had been folded up on a chair and the only thing that I was wearing was my tiny knickers. A white robe hung on the back of the door so I slipped it on. It was quite short and barely covered my thighs. Still a little sleepy and under the influence, I made my entrance into the kitchen where three women stood chatting and laughing. One of them pointed to the coffee pot as to gesture; did I want one?

"Good morning sunshine, how are you feeling now?"

It was Charlie; she had a welcoming smile to greet me with and pulled out a chair at the table for me to sit on. She had been up for hours and looked refreshed in her khaki jeans and tight fitting tee shirt. Her green eyes suited her skin tone and her short dark hair had tiny kiss curls at the back.

"Hi Sarah, do you remember us. You were a bit plastered last night." One of the girls asked me.

"Yes I remember you, Kez and Jules isn't it? Things seem a little fuzzy right now." I sipped on my coffee and tried my best to maintain an image of dignity but I must have looked like a zombie and I started to feel quite nauseous.

"Well let me remind you." Charlie piped up. "First of all I had my eye on you for a while, then I danced with you, then I introduced myself to you in the toilet. Right after we fucked of course."

I spat my coffee out, as I had just taken a rather large sip of it and Jez and Jules burst out laughing. Whilst Charlie maintained a smug grin knowing that she had just embarrassed me.

A feeling of shame came over me at the thought of being picked up and shagged in the toilet and that the event was being replayed in front of her friends.

"Oh don't worry Sarah."Charlie laughed. "We have no secrets

from each other in this house. My friends know exactly what I'm about, and I saw something in you that I liked and I went after it."

"Well there are other ways to pick me up you know. Do I look I have, available please shag me anywhere; written on my face." I smarted off feeling quite annoyed that my personal life was being ridiculed.

"Hey sunshine, I think you've got the wrong idea." She replied in a comforting voice. "It wasn't like that, I couldn't help myself. I wanted you and I had to have you. Now come here and give me some sugar."

Kez and Jules carried on making breakfast, and as I listened to their conversation I noticed that they had a great deal of respect for each other. There was calmness in their voices as they spoke, and tenderness showed between them as they interacted.

"How did you all meet?" I asked watching them all get along in harmony.

Charlie grinned and then told me that she met Jez a few years ago and that they became lovers for several months. But as a couple it just didn't work, so they decided to still live together as house mates. Then when she met Jules it was just sex, sex, sex, and not a lot else. They hadn't been able to form a relationship but did like to hang around each other. Then Jez and Jules had a one night stand and here they all were today.

"Well I think it's nice that you have remained friends all this time." I said with a little confusion.

Jez spoke out as she handed me a plate of toast and asked what my story was. They seemed to be quite concerned when I told them everything that had happened over the last few months. My emotions began to break through as I spoke about Robbie, and how I'd deeply fallen for her. I had to keep stopping in mid sentence and look away for a few seconds just to bring myself back to reality.

Charlie patted my leg gently to reassure me that everything was ok now and that she understood that there was unfinished business in my relationship with Robbie. But I knew in my heart that Robbie would never want to talk to me again.

"Hey you know what." Charlie suddenly called out. "I'm doing a married woman!" She tickled me in my ribs and I almost fell backwards off my chair. "I must admit Sarah." She said with a more serious tone in her voice. "I do find you hot, and you are definitely a trophy wife, and you do turn me on just by looking at you, but I do tend to end up being really good friends with my girlfriends rather than lovers. So if this doesn't work out between us, I promise you, we will have a great relationship."

My inhibitions were beginning to melt, and as I felt a closeness building towards Charlie, she nuzzled her face inside my robe and gave me little nibbles on my shoulder and neck, causing me to have a slight feeling of arousal. I didn't mind the fact that there were two other people in the room with us; I actually found it to be a really big turn on to have an audience, as I'd always fantasised about being watched whilst having sex. But at this point fondling would do.

Charlie sensed that I was becoming sexually interested, so she lifted me up and carried me to her room, where upon throwing me onto her bed she tugged at my robe revealing my protruding nipples and my silky flat stomach, which was rising up and down heavily as my breathing became more intense. She guided my knickers slowly down my legs and used light gentle strokes on my inner thighs, giving me reason to get excited. She knew how to control my body with her hands, and with each thrust she gave, I gave an excited groan of joy. My entire being was in ecstasy and I couldn't hold back the loud cry that bellowed from my mouth as I released my explosive orgasm.

The connection between us was intense, and passionate kissing followed, as we stroked and caressed each other's heated up bodies.

"I want to make you feel good sunshine." She whispered in my ear.

"I'm not sure if I can return the favour Charlie, I don't want you to think that I'm a selfish bitch, I just don't feel right."

"Hell no, you're still in love with Robbie, and for you to commit to me like that would be like betraying her. I do want you to know that I have been known to not fully commit to monogamy, as I've

Chapter Nine: Three Up Two Down

never had good enough reason to. I like girls; a lot, and I tend to go after what I like. You do understand that I will be seeing others don't you?" She was deadly serious about having a bit on the side but I wasn't so sure if I was going to be happy about that.

"Yes Charlie I completely understand." I said thinking that maybe I would be the one to break that nasty little habit.

At that moment Jez knocked on the door and informed Charlie that there was a girl waiting on the phone for her. I felt a small tug of annoyance at this, but Charlie seemed like a free spirit and probably would just hide her infidelity from me if I ever made an issue about it. At least she was being honest with me.

Whilst she was on the phone, Jez stayed in the room with me and she couldn't take her lustful eyes off my slender naked body. I had no problem being on display and even asked her if she liked what she saw.

When Charlie came back in, there was a glance between the two of them, like an understanding of some sort. I immediately recognised what was going to take place and with my consent Jez lifted her top up over her head and threw it to the ground, and as she undid her jeans Charlie beckoned Jules to come to the room. I knew that I was about to enter into an orgy with these girls, and as they both slid onto the bed fully naked, Charlie sat in a chair in the corner and watched us perform pleasures on each other, each one taking it in turn to get sexual gratification. Once we were all spent Charlie joined us for the aftermath of kissing and a little horse play before we all fell asleep until early evening.

CHAPTER TEN

TEAM CHARLIE

*T*he weeks that followed were filled with Charlie's presence. She encouraged me to feel good about myself and even introduced me to a healthier eating habit. We trained at the gym together, and whilst working out we'd eye up the other women giving them marks out of ten on their physical attractiveness; some even scoring a minus on their lack of assets. Saggy asses should be kept indoors not on display!

Being with Charlie gave me a good reason for feeling alive again. We enjoyed each other's company and often included Jez and Jules in our intimate sessions of love making; we had become our own private little family.

I kept no secrets from Jessica and we would swap details on our latest sexual exploits, I even had a feeling that Jen had backed off with her viciousness, as she had stayed clear of any trouble making; to my knowledge anyway.

Life in general was getting better for me; my boss was opening up a new store and had asked me to go into partnership with her. I jumped at the chance of being my own boss, and renovations soon began on our new building. The work didn't take long, and walking in to our newly completed store with brightly lit up neon signage and funky 1960's designs were amazing. I had promoted one of the girls from the other store to be my manager and employed a couple of pretty young things to work part time. The styles of clothing lines that we carried were quite varied, as I wanted to cater for all walks of life, I made sure that we supplied for the more masculine women as well as the pretty princess's that are out there.

Charlie knew a lot of people and would encourage them to shop at the store and we also held a fashion show on Halloween night which made us quite a good penny, so I treated everyone to a night out clubbing.

I danced seductively with Charlie, Jez and Jules, kissing and fondling all three of them, we didn't have to hide what we were to each other as this behaviour was quite acceptable within these walls.

Jessica had started seeing Jen behind Jakes back; they would sneak off to Jens place when Jake was at work or out of town on a business trip. I knew that Jen was completely dominating their relationship and I feared for Jessica's marriage falling into the realms of the divorce statistics. Avoiding Jen's sly remarks was easy for me; I just pretended that she wasn't there. But she did have her uses, I would get drops of information on Robbie's whereabouts and so far I had become privy to knowing that she had her own little pad and was working for Kate as a personal assistant. She was still single which made my heart jump with joy and gave me that butterfly feeling in my stomach which always occurred when she kissed or touched me or even looked at me for that matter.

Charlie understood my need for information on Robbie and would see the sadness in my eyes when I was missing her. She would comfort me and we would talk about Robbie on numerous occasions; keeping her alive inside me, just until I was ready to let her go.

I held great respect for Charlie and I always knew when she had been with another girl; she would think that she had been discreet, but the tell tale signs always came through. She did offer to answer any questions that I had, but I declined as the need to know didn't even enter my head. Jealousy had not played a part in this relationship. There was one occasion when I had gone to the loo in the club and I overheard a girl bragging to her friend that she had gone down on Charlie earlier that day, and that her stupid girlfriend was oblivious to it. I took pride in myself when I waited for them to come out of the cubicle and introduced myself to them as the stupid one, then exited without another word.

I wasn't bothered that I had come face to face with one of Charlie's conquests and I was quite flattered that she had chosen someone who looked similar to me.

We made a good team together as I didn't put a ball and chain around her ankle and she had the freedom to shag whoever she wanted, because deep down we both knew that neither one of us could give our whole heart to each other. Charlie was yet to find that special person and my heart still belonged to another.

The Christmas season was upon us and my parents as usual, wanted me to spend the holidays with them. But I wanted to spend the festivities with Charlie and the girls. It was hard to say no to my Parents, so I compromised and invited Charlie to come with me. I warned her that it was going to be boring and that my parents had no idea about my lifestyle.

Charlie drove us to my parent's house in Bristol, and we made the journey fun by telling corny jokes and attempting to sing songs that we hardly knew the words to. It was dark and beginning to snow when we arrived and as we pulled up in the driveway we beeped the horn several times rather loudly. My parents came running out to greet us and I received a massive warm reception from them both.

"Mum dad, this is Charlie." We fuck get over it; was what I wanted to say.

"Hello Charlie it's so nice to meet you dear." They said giving her a welcoming hug. "Now come in girls we're getting wet from the snow. Where on earth are your jackets? Really you young things just don't know how to look after yourselves."

I looked at Charlie and we sniggered like naughty school children. We plonked our bags in my old room where my parents had set up a second bed next to mine for Charlie to sleep in; little did they know that we were lovers.

Dinner was served and the table was filled with chicken pie and vegetables grown fresh in the garden. Dad opened a bottle of Asti Spumante, mums favourite, and we enjoyed catching up on how things were going with the shop, and how dad had grown this year's vegetable crop quite successfully. Polite questions were put to Charlie, so as to make her feel comfortable in the Niles house of fun.

We retreated into the lounge where the fireplace was filled with burning logs and gave an orange ambience to the room which cre-

Chapter Ten: Team Charlie

ated a cozy atmosphere, and chocolates had been placed in a small glass bowl next to my favourite chair. My mother always knew how to make me feel special.

"Well girls." My mother announced. "Tomorrow is Christmas Eve and there are lots of things for us to do, so we're off to bed now. Good night darling, goodnight Charlie, and don't forget to turn the TV off when you come up."

"Ok we won't." I said; rolling my eyes as if I was ten.

"Night Mr N, Mrs N." Charlie said with a touch of humour.

With the orange glow giving it a romantic feel, we snuggled down together on the sofa and watched the embers of the fire slowly turn to ash and then drifted off to sleep.

My father was the first one to come down the stairs the next morning, and thank god he went straight into the kitchen. I had placed my hand underneath Charlie's top whilst we slept and it was all too obvious what I was feeling. We quickly shot up and turned the TV off and ran to the stairs, being very careful to be quiet. Mum was just coming out of the bathroom so we turned around and pretended that we had just got up by yawning and stretching our arms out and making our voices still sound sleepy.

We went into the kitchen and joined my father for coffee where we were soon joined by my mother who was in a really cheery mood and looked as though she was dressed ready to go out.

"Well girls." She said with a beaming smile, would you like to come shopping with me today? It would be rather handy if Charlie drove us, just so your father can get on with things here."

"Sure mum, I suppose you're waiting to go now." It was the coat and hat in her arms that gave me a clue.

We went into Bristol city centre, where mum had to show Charlie the Cathedral and give her a tour of some of the ancient buildings that were still standing, and even the church, or what was left of it, where my Grandparents had got married in, but it had been destroyed during the war leaving behind just a fraction of its once glorious status.

After shopping for many gifts, we ended up in a small pub by the harbour for lunch. I recognised the girl that served us, as I went to school with her. She was an outed lesbian and when she saw me with Charlie she just knew what I was up to and winked at me. My mother questioned me on why she would do such a thing, so I just passed it off as a friendly gesture. God my parents would have heart failure if they knew their little princess was a slut for pussy.

Evening came and we all placed our gifts under the tree. Apparently my parents had invited some of their friends, including their sons may I add, over for drinks.

The house was filled with the sound of people enjoying their conversations, and chinking their glasses in making toasts to several achievements of the past year. My mother spent most of the evening passing round the sandwiches and crisps, and introducing me and Charlie to several young men in hopes that we might choose one to settle down with; in her wildest dreams.

Though the chat up lines were really lame, we had a lot of fun listening to them and when I told one guy that we were lesbians he asked if he could watch. The answer he got in reply was a subtle; piss off. Charlie and I were definitely the outsiders in this crowd.

Just before midnight we were waving good bye at the door to the last guests to leave and feeling quite merry we all decided to call it a night.

"Would you like your gift now Sarah?" Charlie asked with a huge smile on her face.

"Really can I? I mean, yes." I answered in a flurry.

I opened a long pink velvet box, and wrapped inside pink shredded tissue was a long pink silicone shape. I looked at Charlie questioningly, and then she pulled out her harness from a bag on the floor and said; "I'm hoping you'll say yes."

I had denied her the pleasure that she deserved for far too long, so I allowed her to fit it on me, and I could see the thrilled look on her face as she did so. It was awkward at first and I felt a little stupid, but as we got into the rhythm of it, I started to get more confident at what I was doing, and Charlie had to bury her head in the pillow so my parents couldn't hear her groans of pleasure.

We were at it for hours, and I gained great satisfaction in giving Charlie a good time. The stigma of believing that I was cheating on Robbie no longer existed, and for the first time I was able to let my guard down.

We only managed to get three hours of sleep as my parents were making busy noises downstairs putting the turkey on and phoning everyone, wishing them a merry Christmas. We sneaked into the shower together and as we got over playful and a little noisy, my mother knocked on the bathroom door and asked if everything was alright.

"Yes mum, be down soon promise." I called back to her over the noise of the shower water running.

"Ok sweetheart, prezzies are waiting for you." She replied merrily.

When she had left we wrapped ourselves in towels and ran quickly to my room before she sussed anything was up.

"That was fucking close." I said as I tried to dry myself as fast as I could.

"Will you ever come out to them?" Charlie asked as she patted my back down with her towel.

I gave it some thought for a short moment and answered; "I don't really know how they would take it, I'm not sure if they should know about my sexual preferences. We've never actually had any sort of conversation about gays and lesbians; anyway here I have a gift for you." I changed the subject quickly as I was uncomfortable about the thought of my parents knowing about my carnal knowledge.

I had bought her a white gold dog tag pendant and chain and had it inscribed with; for keeping me safe. It was a tender felt moment between us and I knew that our friendship was going to last forever.

We went down stairs and a greeting of merry Christmas and glasses of champagne were waiting for us. Gifts were exchanged; I had bought my parents an antique clock to hang on the wall in the hallway. This went down well as they had it on their, to buy list. I received a gold watch and a matching necklace with a heart shaped diamond hanging from it. Charlie got a pink fleecy jumper and a silver bracelet with tiny diamantes over it.

She thanked them quite gracefully out of respect, but pink definitely wasn't in Charlie's nature and I knew she hated it on herself. We enjoyed the rest of the day together, eating plenty of festive food and filled up on the finest Belgian chocolates.

During the afternoon my mother asked Charlie if there was a man in her life. There was hesitation in her answer, and then she informed my mother that she had never had a boyfriend. My mother thought this was odd and commented on how beautiful she was and that men must surely be falling at her feet.

"I've never been interested in boys to be honest Mrs N." She said and then winked at me.

I stared at Charlie as if to say don't give any more information, and tapped her foot with mine as I asked her to pass me the chocolates. My annoyance began to show and I tried to shove the sweets into her mouth to shut her up.

"So do you always wear boots like that Charlie." My mother asked staring at her footwear.

"Oh yes I love my boots Mrs N, I have a couple of pairs like these."

"Don't they hurt your feet dear? Maybe you should get some shoes like Sarah's, that'll help you catch a boy I'm sure. And Sarah, should I ask if there's such a thing as a boyfriend your life. You never seem to introduce us to any of them." Shit now I was on the spot.

I could feel myself going red with embarrassment as I wanted to tell them, but it was the hardest thing to find the right words to say. So I lied.

"No mum I have no time for men at all, I mean being busy with the shop and everything." My fingers were crossed behind my back; a habit I had as a child whenever I told a fib to my parents.

Chapter Ten: Team Charlie

Charlie gave a small laugh and then put her arms around my waist just before she kissed me on my cheek and said. "Sarah maybe it would be a good idea if you just tell them the truth and get it out in the open once and for all."

"No I can't Charlie!" I snapped at her annoyed that she was so pushy. "I just can't, they won't understand, it's not right."

"Just say it sunshine." She whispered in my ear.

So I just blurted it out. "I'm a lesbian, and so is Charlie."

My mother's jaw dropped in shock, and I could see the stunned look on both of their faces.

"I'm with Charlie, we're together; you know a couple. We're an item." I stammered as I struggled to get the right words to come out of my mouth.

My father put his arm around my mother to comfort her as her voice went into high pitch mode as she screeched. "You're gay? You're both gay? But how did this happen and grandchildren what about grandchildren?"

"Mum listen, I've never wanted children. I...I...Charlie help me."

Charlie took control of the conversation, and in a calm sympathetic voice made her speech; "I think what Sarah's trying to say is that for a long time she was miserable and now she's not."

"Is that it?" I was surprised at the lack of defending on my behalf. "I thought you would have had more to say than that Charlie. I think what Charlie's trying to say, or rather, I am, is that…"

I grabbed Charlie's hand and pulled her in towards me, giving her a great big wet kiss on the lips, and then as I pulled away from her I looked at my parents and said. "This is what I want!"

My parents stood in shock, with not much to say, apart from my mother stating that she needed another drink.

I pleaded my case so they could see my side and not be prejudice. "I'm still the same person that you've always loved, and I hope you still do. I'm not going to live my life any other way; it's proved to me that it just doesn't work for me."

"Well I must be honest with you girls." My father said softly.

"We're not disappointed in you at all, either of you. We just don't know how we're supposed to respond to all of this information."

Charlie squeezed my hand tightly and said. "You had better tell them the rest sunshine."

I got them to sit down and poured more wine into my mother's glass so she could absorb the shock of what I was about to say. I informed them that I had got married in the spring, to a total stranger, who happened to be a woman from Canada. Then I fell in love with her, then we broke up because of another woman, and soon we can apply to get divorced. As I summed my life up, I could hear how stupid it all sounded, but I had to tell them everything.

"Is this why you were in such a state when we came over dear?" It had suddenly dawned on my mother the reasoning for my depression and why she was unable to help me at that time in my life.

"Yes mum, I really couldn't tell you at the time, you do understand don't you?"

"So what's this woman's name?" My father asked and he didn't look too impressed with the way that I had been treated by her either. After all was it not me who had saved her ass when she needed the help.

"Her name is Robbie." I said, still getting emotional at the sound of it.

Charlie passed me a tissue and comforted me by stroking my back with gentle circular movements. The thought quickly ran through my mind of wondering where she had spent Christmas, maybe she went to Kate's.

"So we have a daughter in law now." My mother pointed out. "Is that everything? Or are there anymore secrets you need to tell us about?"

"I'm not pregnant if that's a bonus." I joked trying to lift the atmosphere.

My parents left the room and went into the kitchen to do the washing up. Really they wanted to be alone so that they could discuss my situation.

Chapter Ten: Team Charlie

"Well I think they handled that really well." Charlie said quite proud of herself.

"I know! I can't believe I've told them everything." A surge of relief ran through me and I felt like life was treating me to an extra Christmas present this year.

"I'm pleased for you sunshine, you don't have to hide your emotions around them anymore. Now I'm still in shock that I'm wearing pink, I feel like such a dork."

We finished the day by sending all of our friends text messages, wishing them a happy crimbo, and I also sent one to Kate and included Robbie's name in the merriment. I had a secret wish that she would text me back, but for now I focused my thoughts on what I had.

When my parents returned from the kitchen, they had been discussing all the gay people they knew of and relayed their names back to us. It was interesting to know that they had paid such attention to non heterosexual relationships. I had no idea that my parents really were cool trendy people.

CHAPTER ELEVEN

A FAVOUR FOR ROBBIE

*T*he next morning we ate breakfast with my parents, and their acceptance on my life style was pleasing to see.

We chatted and laughed for a while and then it was time to make our way back to London. My mother would always get upset when I left, so I liked to keep my goodbyes short with her. She filled a box with festive goodies for us to eat on our journey home and as we drove off the tears were spilling down her cheeks.

"Your parents are so cool." Charlie remarked as we drove off. "I can't believe they didn't freak out."

I had images of them sitting on the sofa sipping tea and saying well the signs were there, and I already knew it.

As Charlie was driving, I placed my hand on her leg in appreciation and said in a humble manor. "Thank you Charlie, for being there for me I mean. So what about your parents? Do you see much of them?" She had never mentioned her family and I felt like such a shit for never asking her about her background.

"No I don't they turned their backs on me when I came out, my friends are my family now." She kept her eyes focused on the road and didn't look fazed by the conversation.

"I'm sorry to hear that." I said feeling quite sad for her. "Maybe they'll come round to the idea in time."

"It's been years sunshine, I think the path they're on is leading in a different direction to mine. It's ok; I came to terms with that a long time ago."

I felt really pissed off at this news and stuck my head out of the car window and shouted out. "Why the fuck can't people just come to terms with the fact that there are feelings being hurt when they refuse to accept another human beings way of life." At least it entertained Charlie.

Chapter Eleven: A Favour for Robbie

Jez and Jules were at home when we arrived and they were looking a little worse for wear. They had been out partying till the early hours and had over done it with the alcohol.

Jessica was having a party that night and I invited the girls to come with me. It was obvious why Jez and Jules couldn't face going, and Charlie passed on the invite as she was exhausted from driving, but she urged me to go anyway. I gave all three of them a passionate kiss each before leaving to go to my apartment to get ready. Charlie had offered to drive me but I could see that she was too tired, and the walk wasn't so bad.

The party was in full swing when I got to Jessica's and the house was packed with people drinking and eating. Jake appeared in front of me and put a glass of wine in my hand.

"Jessica's in the conservatory go on through." He said pointing her out amongst the gathered guests.

"Thanks Jake and cheers." I made my way through the crowd to find my friend.

Jessica spotted me and gave me an approving look. "Hey babe you look fucking amazing."

"Thanks Jessica, you look pretty hot yourself. Who are all these people?"

"Oh some are Jakes acquaintances and some are Jens." She commented looking around, not knowing most of the people herself.

"So you're still in with her then?" I answered her with a disapproving look.

"She keeps our sex life alive, and Jake enjoys watching us together." Well lucky Jake getting his rocks off at someone else's expense.

"So what Jake wants, Jake gets does he?" I snapped at her. But I really wanted to spit in his face.

She in turn snapped back at me. "Jake wanted you, but you weren't available, and I'm not ready to lose him just yet."

"Ok I'll back off, I'm sorry for not having more faith in you." Wow I hadn't realised that she felt so strongly about this.

I sensed that our friendship was changing as we were slowly growing apart. But as a true friend I wasn't going to give up on her. I stayed for a while trying to mingle with the guests but I noticed that some of them kept disappearing into the bedroom. It was obvious that acts of a sexual nature were going on but my interest was short lived so I made my excuses and left.

I decided to go back to Charlie's and spend the evening with her, but when I walked into her bedroom I found she wasn't alone. There were clothes scattered all over the floor and two naked bodies fumbling around beneath the bed sheets.

"Oh Charlie, I'm really sorry, I didn't mean to interrupt you like that. I'll go and I'll call you tomorrow. Bye and bye whatever your name is." I quickly exited and made my way down the stairs as fast as I could and I was shortly chased by a naked and surprised Charlie.

"Sarah wait, you weren't supposed to be here tonight." She cried out as she reached for my shoulder and stopped me from running any further.

"It's ok Charlie, honest, I'm to blame for the embarrassment caused here. We have a deal and I'm fine with it. You are my friend as well as my lover and I want you to be happy more than anything. Now go back upstairs and give what's her name a good time. Go, please." I was actually fine with the whole situation and I wanted her to know that.

"Sarah you're the best." She said acknowledging that I was right.

I walked off down the street chanting the word; fuck, fuck, fuck. Seeing Charlie with another woman didn't bother me in the least, I was all for it, but not knowing when she was going to be conquering another territory made it a little embarrassing when faced with the ordeal.

I was on the phone to her the next morning and I couldn't apologise enough for acting like such an ass. She was concerned about me and wanted to know if I was ok and not too spooked by it all.

"I'll see you tonight then." I said, making sure to confirm that there were no hidden surprises on the horizon.

Chapter Eleven: A Favour for Robbie

I had a full busy day at the store catching up with inventory and changing the outfits on the mannequins to create a fab new window display. It was when I put a shirt up on a hanger to drape in the background that a familiar voice spoke behind me. "Hello Sarah." She said softly. I thought I was going to melt on the spot; before I even turned around I knew it was Robbie. My heart lifted; engulfed with delight as I saw her face looking at me. She was breathtaking and really here.

"Robbie, hi how are you? You look great." She looked amazing and those beautiful blue eyes, how I'd missed them.

"I'm fine I suppose." She held her head low and having a knack for picking up on inner emotions I could sense that she was uneasy.

"Well I hear you're working for Kate now, that's nice." I began to play with my hair like a stupid school girl having her first crush but my fingers were working overtime as my nerves were setting in so I started to lean in for that big emotional welcome back kiss but I hadn't accounted for Robbie's response or lack of it; leaving me in mid pucker.

There was an awkward pause between us and I became aware that something was amiss. One of the girls in the store called for my assistance so I asked Robbie if she could wait a moment. She told me that she was in a rush but could we meet up in the morning at the coffee shop.

"Yes sure." I said grinning like a Cheshire cat. "You really caught me by surprise; I really look forward to seeing you tomorrow." Stay calm and act natural I told myself as I watched her walk away; my heart was pounding and my mind was racing.

Talking to Charlie about it that evening was easy, we even involved Jez and Jules in the conversation. Jez reckoned that she was going to ask for a divorce, but I sensed somehow that it was something else. Charlie thought that she had finally come to her senses and was going to ask me to get back with her. God was it so wrong for me to want that so much?

I spent the night with Charlie, but sex wasn't on the agenda, we stayed up for hours talking about what exactly we wanted from each other, and Charlie was a firm believer in going after what she wanted and that that was not going to change with me. I loved her in a special way that I could love no other, but neither of us was actually in love with each other.

The next morning I awoke early so that I could spend plenty of time getting ready. I chose a tight black T shirt to wear with my white jeans. All of my curves showed off in all the right places and if she didn't find me hot in this get up then she must be mad.

She was already there when I arrived, so I brushed myself down and checked my reflection out in the window and then went inside to greet her. I shook her hand and kissed her on the cheek in a very formal manner keeping everything on a professional level.

"You look really good Sarah, I see you have some nice muscle tone happening there." Yeah she had noticed my new qualities.

"Yes, thanks for noticing. After you, I mean, when we went our separate ways I turned all my energy towards the gym. I still work out there a couple of times a week and a friend comes with me." Maybe she was my lover and the person who opened my closet door to my parents but Robbie didn't have to know that.

"Well that's good." Her voice was soft and inviting and it was good standing in her presence; it made me feel warm and tingly.

"So may I ask what brings us here today Robbie? I am intrigued." I crossed my legs and placed my hands over my knee to look business like and professional, and of course, seductive but she looked really serious and there was sadness in her eyes.

"Sarah I have something important to ask you and I completely understand if you can't do it. My mother has been seriously hurt in a car accident and I have to fly back home tomorrow. I'm not sure how long I'll be away for and this is where I have a proposition for you." How awful for her I couldn't possibly imagine how she must be feeling right now.

"Ok I'm listening." I leaned in closer towards her and gave her my complete attention.

She put her hand on the table as if she was reaching out for my

Chapter Eleven: A Favour for Robbie

assurance and I really wanted to grab it and hold on to it like a starved sex maniac.

"My proposition is; would you be able to keep an eye on Kate for me? She doesn't trust too many people and I know that she has a soft spot for you. Please say no if you want to, I do understand, especially after the way we parted company. But no one else can be trusted." Tears were building up in her eyes and her desperation showed and knowing that she had so little time to make alternate arrangements how could I possibly leave her feeling deprived. My heart went out to her and all I could think about was the pain that she must be in.

"Yes Robbie, of course I will, you don't have to worry about Kate I will take good care of her you can count on that." I sipped on my cappuccino and assured her that there was nothing to worry about.

"I'm sorry about the way things have turned out between us Sarah." She said as she gently brushed her finger across the top of my lip to remove the coffee foam that had been left behind.

There was a moment of kindness and for one instance I thought that there might possibly be a chance for us. Her eyes welled up with tears again making my heart melt for her and this was the first time I'd witnessed her weakness break through; I was going to support her no matter what.

"Robbie I haven't stopped loving you." The words came out so fast that there was no time to stop myself from saying them.

"I really can't get into that right now Sarah." She replied coolly. "Maybe we can talk when I get back."

I realised that my timing was pretty lousy and selfish, so I thanked her for choosing me to help out and wished her mum a healthy quick recovery. She thanked me again for helping out at such short notice and told me that I was an amazing person.

"I have to go now and get ready to leave. Kate will have my contact number in case of emergencies and here's a set of keys so you can let yourself in. I'm really grateful Sarah; I'll be in touch soon." At that we stood up and hugged, I wanted to squeeze her tightly and never let her go, but this meeting wasn't about my needs at all.

We didn't take our eyes off each other as she made her exit out of the doorway and I watched her walk down the street until she was out of my sight.

It was hard seeing her go after such a short meeting and I was feeling a little deflated from my expectations of something more. But I was a trooper and helping Kate out was my pleasure.

After talking to Charlie about my situation she vowed to help me in any way that she could to win Robbie's heart back. Although this was going to prove to be difficult, being as we had been apart for so long and the fact that Robbie was going to be in another country indefinitely.

I made arrangements at the store with staff coverage and also texted Jessica to let her know what was happening and that my time spent with her would be a little limited for the time being.

CHAPTER TWELVE

BONDING WITH KATE

I arrived at Kate's later that evening and let myself in. She greeted me with open arms and we chatted for ages swapping information on the past few months. I told her all about Charlie and how good she was to me, and of Jessica's set up with Jen. Kate knew how Jen worked on people with her controlling ways and advised me to steer well clear of her.

She had also been trying to persuade Robbie to see sense on her relationship with me but all she could get out of her was that she couldn't allow herself to get hurt again. I began to feel that Robbie's stubbornness had caused her to miss out on something that could have been so wonderful.

I cooked us a supper of salmon and rice under Kate's supervision and made sure she had everything she needed for the night, before returning back to Charlie's.

Things were moving forward for me, and Charlie could see that as a couple we were coming to a standstill. That night was to be the last that we would be intimate, we were more passionate than we had ever been, and I felt a slight sadness as we held each other tightly all night long. We promised that no matter what, our friendship would stay strong forever.

I had invited Charlie to tag along with me to meet Kate, and as I cooked breakfast she and Kate hit it off like a storm. I left the two of them chatting whilst I went off to get some supplies in. I was gone a couple of hours and came back to the two of them making plans for a girl's night out. Kate hadn't been out for ages and I heard a strip club mentioned.

I interrupted their conversation quite sharply as I peered around the corner of the doorway.

"Strip club, I've never been to a strip club."

"Oh Sarah, I can't believe you've never been to one. Charlie; are you free on Saturday night?"

Kate started to laugh as she knew I had missed out on a lot of fun. A feeling of naivety came over me as I had played the princess bitch for so long, that I had forgotten that there was so much more out there than what revolved around my little world. Charlie offered to round up Jez and Jules and we arranged to meet at Kate's at 7.30pm on Saturday night.

"I'm not sure if I should go you guys." I whined. "It's not something I've ever thought about."

"Are you shitting me girl." Charlie asked in surprise. "This is for your benefit. We're not taking no for an answer! Tell her Kate." She was adamant that I was going and being outnumbered by two to one didn't give much room for my argument.

"You must go you'll have fun I promise." She said reassuringly.

"But Kate I'm supposed to be looking after you!"

"No buts, it's all arranged, you're going." She laughed; hinting that she had a wicked sense of humour.

After lunch we left Kate to take her usual afternoon nap and went back to Charlie's, where we didn't even have to do too much enticing to get the girls to come with us. They were more than well up for it.

Saturday came and we all made our way round to Kate's and had a few drinks before heading off to the club. It was mostly filled with dirty old men leering at the girls dancing on the stage. We sat at a table near to the front and joined in with the cheering and whistling. Our server Natasha looked after us all night, making sure that our glasses were permanently topped up.

As I looked around the club, I spotted a face that I recognised; standing in the shadows almost in the darkness was that bloody bitch Jen. She was dressed in PVC hot pants and bra, and as the music changed she made her way up onto the stage. She grabbed the pole and climbed up it then swung round lifting her legs up into the air as she did. Her moves were well thought out and I could see the en-

Chapter Twelve: Bonding with Kate

joyment on her face as she showed off her act to her captivated audience. Her eyes were constantly fixated on the same spot in the crowd, as if she was dancing for someone in particular. I followed the line to where she was looking and was astounded to see Jake sitting there with someone on his lap and she wasn't Jessica.

I nudged Charlie's arm and told her that Jessica's husband was in the club. He had his hands all over this woman and his tongue was dancing down her throat. When Jen had finished her number the crowd applauded and gave her major tips as she moved between the tables and teased her onlookers before making her way over to Jake. He then proceeded to pluck the cash out from her bra as she leaned in to kiss him and then straight after she immediately focused her attentions on kissing this other woman; to the point of sexually arousing her.

I wanted to know where Jessica was so I sent her a text asking if she was ok and how were things going with Jake. She replied right back saying that Jake was on a business trip and she was getting ready for his return.

He was up to no good, business trip my fucking arse. My natural instinct kicked in to protect my friend's honour probing me to investigate the matter a little more diligently, so I walked straight over to his table, closely followed by Charlie and confronted him.

"So I thought you were on a business trip Jake, I see you're out with the forever pleasant Jen and this slut." My adrenaline was building up forcing me to get even angrier at them.

He looked a little surprised to see me and I could see his mind was working overtime trying to think of an excuse but the dumb shit wasn't clever enough to come up with anything. Jen smiled and took hold of his hand and started to lick it like the horny bitch that she was.

"Hey sexy it's been a while, care to join in the fun with us?" She said knowing that she was getting right up my nose.

I rolled my eyes in annoyance whilst looking directly at Jake and answered her back quite snappishly. "Oh piss off Jen, if I want to talk to a bitch I'll call in the dog catchers."

I could tell that the slut who was with them wanted to smack me one, but Charlie; my hero; was there to protect me.

"So Jake, what's going on? Why did you lie to Jessica? After all you're the one who talked her into having a threesome and now you're being deceitful, is there something you want tell me?" What a piece of lousy crap he's turned out to be.

"Umm Sarah I…"

"Save it Jake! You're nothing but a wanker." I barked, quickly interrupting his pathetic performance. "And you Jen, when the fuck are you going to disappear?"

She looked at me with such evilness on her face and then stroked Jakes hair like he was her puppy. "I told you when I first met you Sarah that I don't go away that easily. Jake can make up his own mind who he wants to fuck. Look at this girl; she's so hot I can't wait to taste her myself and besides little wifey is where she belongs; at home!"

I stared at the three of them in dismay and felt such disgust at what they were doing behind my friend's back.

I could feel my heart pound harder as I whispered into Jakes ear. "Perhaps I should mention to Jessica that I saw you here tonight, I'm sure she'd be pretty interested to know." The silent assassin inside me was ready to leap out and grab him by his balls but I had to contain myself from doing any physical harm so instead I pulled out my phone and took a snapshot of the sleazy three. Jake tried to grab it from me but Jen pulled him back in hope that Jessica would find out the truth.

Charlie took me by the arm and managed to coax me back to the others, and as I was explaining what was going on, my voice went into high pitch mode like a chicken on speed. We all agreed that there was nothing that we could do about it at that point so we carried on spending the evening as best we could.

Different girls took their turn and confidently performed their teasing sexual acts seducing the pole, each one trying to outshine the other before collecting their hard earned tips from the excited onlookers who were desperately trying to get their favourite dancer's attention by paying for it.

Chapter Twelve: Bonding with Kate

Jessica had been on my mind all evening, and talking to her the next morning, I found that matters had only worsened. Jake hadn't returned home that evening and even had the nerve to send her a message pretending that he was still stuck in Italy.

Whilst she made coffee I went into the bathroom and phoned Jens number so I could speak to Jake and persuade him to come home. But when she answered her phone I could hear a lot of giggling in the background and then the words fuck off were screamed at me shortly before being cut off.

Jessica called out that the coffee was made and when I returned she asked me who I was just talking to. I couldn't think of an excuse and to be honest I didn't want to, so I had no choice but to show her the picture I had taken at the club. The happiness that had surrounded her naive little world disappeared in seconds as the realisation that Jake was totally cheating on her hit hard.

She stared at the picture for ages as tears of anger and hurt were building up in her eyes but I came to find out that the tears were not for Jake, but for Jen. They too had been secretly seeing each other when Jake was away and Jen had promised her that they would soon be exclusive in their relationship.

That snake had suckered Jessica into believing her lies, when she really couldn't be loyal to anyone.

She told me that she had first included Jen into the bedroom to keep Jake happy, as he had claimed that their sex life was becoming stale; which was total bullshit considering the short amount of time they had been together. Also Jen had made Jake aware that his wife was seductive and sexy, and it made her feel good to be noticed by him for a while. But her attentions towards Jen soon became obsessive, so much in fact that she couldn't stand it whenever she had to drop her knickers for Jake anymore.

But to be honest I don't think that Jake had ever cared for Jessica, not in the way that he should have. Why did he ask her to marry him almost as soon as I dumped him? He never acknowledged her much when he was with me and when he did it was to tell her to piss off, so that he could get his rocks off with me.

She put her head on my shoulder as I comforted her and I began to remember the hurt that I felt when Robbie left me. The sadness always seemed to find its way back into my heart and I wondered if I was ever going to truly recover.

I watched her fall asleep on the sofa and stroked her arm to give her reassurance that at least I cared. After waiting around for a while and seeing that she was settled for the night, I made a quiet exit and headed off to Kate's.

I told Kate all about the latest poisonous tricks that Jen had acted out and how sleazy Jake had become. It made me shudder to think of what he was up to behind my back when we were together. But I had come a long way in my life over the past few months, changing from a cold heartless cow to a mellowed out, still hot, woman with a purpose and lots of great new friends. For once I was glad to be me.

As soon as morning arrived Kate suggested that we go for a walk being as the weather was nice and she needed to get some exercise. We had an interesting outing, visiting art galleries and antique stores and strolled across Tower Bridge watching the tourists pass underneath on their boat excursions. It was hard to imagine that a long time ago there used to be houses right where we stood.

It was really easy bonding with Kate and I could see why Robbie fell for her. But it would never be that way for me as she was too girly in her ways and I now knew that my type was the more toned and athletic built.

"Do you think that Robbie will call soon?" I asked her in hope that she'd be able to supply me with a specific day and time.

She looked at me and smiled sweetly as if she knew where I was going with this.

"I'll give it a day or two and if I haven't heard anything I'll send her an email. I think she's probably got her hands full right now."

Oh why was I such a stupid idiot, constantly thinking of my own needs, when she was out there all by herself dealing with trauma? Images of her sitting at her mother's bedside desperate for her to recover flashed through my mind and I could only empathize with how awful it must be for her right now.

Chapter Twelve: Bonding with Kate

"Yes, right, that was a bit thoughtless of me. I do hope that her mother is going to be ok." I answered rather sheepishly.

She informed me that although Robbie is an amazing person she does tend to have a dark side. If she gets into a deep funk when things go wrong for her it takes her a long time to snap out of it. She also told me that she had been saying things in my defence to Robbie to soften the situation, but I had made that a little harder to do when I fucked it all up with Jen.

She quickly changed the subject by asking how things were going with Charlie. I told her that our relationship as lovers was over but that we would be friends for life. I also came clean about the orgies we'd had and how my sexual training had given me the confidence to be a caring lover rather than just being the one who takes.

I knew Kate had a fascination with Charlie, as she too could see the resemblance to Robbie. But I felt it was more on the friendship side and not anything deeper. With Charlie's ability in being compassionate and strong, it was no wonder that she could attract friendships from all walks of life.

CHAPTER THIRTEEN

JESSICA'S BIG NEWS

Over the course of the next few days I shared myself with being a help to Kate, making sure that Jessica was ok and finding time to spend with Charlie. It was tiring but the rewards far outweighed that.

Jessica had kicked Jake out and refused to have anything more to do with Jen. Her emotions were all over the place, she was beginning to go through self loathing and was completely ashamed of herself, and I had to be there for her to pick up the pieces.

I had just arrived at Kate's and saw that she was talking on the phone, so I waved and mouthed to her that I would be in the kitchen. She acknowledged me by waving back and then carried on saying uh huh, yep, and ok. Whilst I was putting the groceries away she walked in holding the phone in her hand.

"It's for you." Her voice was serious as she offered it to me.

"Who is it?" I asked in surprise and took it from her.

I cleared my throat and put on my business voice. "Hello, this is Sarah speaking, how can I help you?"

"Hi, it's Robbie." Her sad voice spoke quietly and I just wanted to go to her. But my heart jumped as a sudden rush of unexpected excitement ran through my body. I had to play it cool and not sound too eager. "How is your mother doing?" There that was mature.

She gave a large sigh before she answered. "The doctors have said that they don't think she is going to make it." Her speech was slow and broken and I could tell that she hadn't had much sleep because she was sounding a little croaky. I wanted to be there for her, to hold her, giving her the security of knowing that I would take care of her.

"God I'm really sorry, is there anything I can do to help? Just name it, I'll do it."

"It's ok Sarah you're already helping me by looking after Kate. That's a big enough responsibility for you. She's all the family I've got right now."

I felt saddened by that remark as I thought she would have included me as family as well. But then she had known Kate for a long time and I had only been in her life for five minutes.

I replied by saying. "I think she's happy with me, she hasn't complained yet about my cooking."

"Oh you're cooking now, no more takeouts for you then. That's good to hear. Listen there's something I want to say…." There was an awkward momentary pause and I could hear her breathing as if she was in turmoil of what she was going to tell me.

"Say what Robbie." I needed to hear what she was going to say.

"Oh it doesn't matter it can wait, I have to go now the doctor is calling me. Take care Sarah and thank you again."

"Take care Robbie, my heart is with you." It always has been.

As our conversation was ended I looked at Kate with big puppy dog eyes. "She wanted to say something to me but she got called away what do you think it could be?"

Kate flapped her arms and had a blank look on her face. "I have no idea Sarah, let's hope it's something good, but also don't forget what she is going through right now." She was losing her mother as we spoke and my selfish heart had taken over for just a short moment. I really was a thoughtless bitch.

"Ok I won't. Kate can I ask you a question? A personal one I mean."

"Yes sure go ahead you can ask me anything."

I looked out of the window and drew in a deep breath. "Why didn't you marry Robbie?"

"That's because I'm still married to someone. Long before I met Robbie I didn't know what I was about, you know the confusion on why do I like girls so much. Anyhow, I met this guy and it was a short lived romance that went sour almost as soon as he put the ring on my finger. I realised that I wanted to be with women and he suffered major embarrassment with his work colleagues and his family, so he moved away."

"So why didn't you get a divorce?" I asked with such naivety.

"The time it would have taken to do that, and I have no idea where on earth he is. The only reason Robbie was so determined to stay at short notice was to look after me. My family disowned me when I came out to them, so I would have been left on my own. I feel guilty enough for being such a burden to people, but my strength is coming back now so I can do more for myself."

Families are real shits! I was lucky that my parents had accepted my lifestyle so easily and that they adored Charlie.

I viewed Kate as a very intellectual woman, very sexy in her appearance, and a completely understanding nature. She makes you feel welcome as soon as she meets you and isn't big headed just because she owns her own business, and she has managed to keep her professional affairs separate from her personal ones.

We decided to have a girl's night in and invited Charlie and Jessica to join us as the two of them hadn't met each other yet.

Charlie was the first to arrive bringing with her a large brown paper bag containing a selection of Chinese food from our local favourite joint. She was shortly followed by Jessica who was clanking two bottles of wine together.

As introductions were made, I could see that Charlie was showing an interest in Jessica, and Jessica god bless her was totally oblivious to it. We all sat around the table and drank plenty with our meals although Jessica stuck to drinking water and we started to share stories of our past sexual experiences, good and bad. Jessica was reluctant to join in at first but we soon convinced her otherwise.

Kate was interested in listening to Jessica's story and probed her further with questions. "So Jessica, where do you plan to go with your life now?" She asked.

"Well I'm not really sure but when the baby is born..."

"What baby?" I shouted out as I spilled my drink straight down my cleavage.

Chapter Thirteen: Jessica's Big News

"Yes, I found out this morning and I'm about eight weeks along." She announced. "And Jake doesn't know about it and I want to keep it that way ok."

I got up and ran round the table to her and held her tightly not knowing if this was good news or bad.

"Oh my god Jessica, you are going to keep it aren't you?"

"Yes I am Sarah, thank you for asking, but I am going to have to find a new place to live."

I offered my services in any way that she needed them in looking for a new apartment, and Charlie started to real off a list of vacant places that she knew of.

We were all in mid conversation when Kate spoke out and said. "Jessica I know of the perfect place for you and the baby. Go and look upstairs, there's a perfect home for you up there. You'll have total privacy and the only room you'd have to share with me is the kitchen. Go and have a look if you want to."

Jessica practically ran upstairs and we could hear her calling out as she went from room to room. "This is great, oh my god this bathroom's huge."

She came downstairs and accepted the offer immediately, giving Kate a hug and a kiss on the cheek as she did so. We all held our glasses in the air and made a toast to new beginnings and also to Jessica's unnoticeable bump.

The alcohol was starting to make me slur my words and talk a complete load of crap. I was laughing at things that weren't even funny, and when the phone rang I jumped up quickly to answer it; tripping over the chair leg and falling straight onto my ass as I did so.

"Hello this is the pissed up bitches residence how can I help you?" I giggled as I looked at the others who just happened to be laughing at my predicament.

"Hi it's Robbie. Is that you Sarah?" I gained a sudden urge to grow the fuck up. How could I have been so insensitive and immature?

"Um yes it is, how are you and how's your mother?" I tried to form my words into sentences but it was harder than I thought.

The silence was enough to let me know the situation, and hearing her heavy breathing from her sad loss gave me great pain in my heart.

"She died earlier this morning." She whispered and then gave a huge sigh.

"Robbie I'm so sorry. Is there anything I can do?" The girls were laughing in the background and I had to put my hand over the speaker and tell them to be quiet.

"Do you have someone there to be with right now?" I asked in hope that some member of her family would be present.

"Yeah please don't worry about me Sarah I'll be ok. Could you put Kate on the phone for me? I need to speak to her."

All I heard Kate say was uh huh and then she left the room. I was a little put out by this as I felt that I should have been a part of this conversation. But Charlie grabbed my hand and held it tightly.

"It'll be ok Sarah they have a lot of history together, don't let this get to you." These were wise words from a wise person.

"I know Charlie; it's just that I don't like being shut out when I feel that I have a place in this circle."

When Kate finally returned back to us she couldn't look me straight in the eyes. I was hungry for the slightest bit of information and the need to know was causing me to feel edgy.

She informed us that Robbie would be returning shortly after her mother's funeral. She just had a few loose ends to tie up, such as putting the family home on the market.

The atmosphere had died down and when Jessica said that she had better make a move Charlie offered to accompany her. As they were leaving Kate reminded Jessica that she was welcome to move in any time.

We watched them walk up the street until they were safely in the car and waved frantically as they drove past. Kate put her hand on my shoulder and gave it a light rub.

Chapter Thirteen: Jessica's Big News

"Are you ok Sarah? You seem to be a little quiet." She suggested we have another drink and toast to life and all it entails.

"Oh I'm ok; it's just been an eventful night that's all."

I fetched us another bottle of wine from the fridge, as we had sobered up a little and while I topped up our glasses Kate told me that she was sorry for walking out of the room when she was talking to Robbie; it was requested because she was too upset and could hear all the laughter in the background.

I understood that Robbie must be feeling pretty shit right now and I also knew that my visits with Kate were going to be less once she was back. So I told her that it was a really generous offer to invite Jessica to live upstairs and she replied by saying that that girl reminded her of her former self and that she needed a fresh start to happiness.

I ended up staying the night after we had watched a soppy love story on TV and the wine had done its job and put me into a deep dreamy sleep.

The next morning I was rudely awoken by my phone ringing. "Sarah hi you're never going to guess what happened last night. When I got home Jake was waiting outside for me and he was really aggressive. So Charlie stepped in and told him to lay off me because the stress could harm the baby. He knows! He fucking knows Sarah!"

"Ok you need to remain calm." I said trying to think logical with a hangover. "He would have found out eventually anyway. The main thing is are you ok? And Charlie how is she?" My head was swimming as I was trying to absorb the information.

"Oh I'm fine in myself, I just feel a little unnerved about Jake. I have no idea what he's going to plan next. And Charlie stayed the night; I was too scared to be on my own in case that jerk came back and tried to do something stupid. She stood up to that bastard for me, she's my hero."

"Yes she's good like that; she tends to have a way that makes you feel safe when she's around. I do think that she has a soft spot for you though."

There was a nervous short laugh just before Jessica completely broke down and admitted that she actually found it difficult to accept that being pregnant was beautiful. I reassured her that she possessed something that even I was jealous of and she should concentrate on her health not her image, as vanity has always been a strong point in her personality but I knew that my reasoning was probably falling on deaf ears.

Over the next few weeks we all took turns in keeping Jessica safe. Jake was making a nuisance of himself as predicted by harassing her whenever she went out, but her ability to be stubborn paid off when she didn't acknowledge him. Her friendship with Charlie grew stronger and I could see that there was a deeper connection evolving from it. Charlie hadn't even looked at another woman; totally out of character and Jessica was besotted by her.

CHAPTER FOURTEEN

ROBBIE'S BACK AND SHE BROUGHT BAGGAGE

*O*n my way over to visit Kate one morning I picked up an assortment of fresh cream cakes and a large bunch of carnations to replace the ones I had let die in the kitchen window: I had intended on numerous occasions to replace them but never got around to it. I called out to Kate that it was me coming in and that I had bought treats but when she heard me come in she summoned me into the lounge where she was sat at the computer going through her emails.

"Hi Sarah, you might want to come and read this, I have some good news for you." Her smile was beaming and she pointed to a chair for me to bring over to place next to hers. I sat down beside her to see what was so important and saw there was a message from Robbie saying that she was coming home. My heart skipped a beat, and a nervous excited sensation took control of my emotions as I read that she was coming home today. She would be back in twenty four hours and arriving at gate three at 5.30pm.

"But this was sent yesterday!" I shrilled as I read the message a second time.

"Yes Sarah, that means that she'll be here in three and a half hours. Do you feel up to coming with me to pick her up?"

I couldn't contain myself; I had no idea what response I would get from Robbie. If she welcomed me with open arms I would know that I stood a second chance and could work on the rest of the situation later. But for now I had to remain calm and poised if I was going to get anywhere and adding any more drama to the emotional torrent that she had just gone through was definitely not on my agenda.

"Do you think that she'll want me there Kate? After all she is just expecting you to wait here isn't she?" Oh god I couldn't wait to see her again.

"She knows me better than that, I always like to meet her at the airport, its fun and I wouldn't have it any other way." She said proudly.

I arranged for Charlie to take us in her car and Jessica just happened to tag along for the ride. We all managed to squeeze in comfortably making sure that there was enough room for Robbie on the journey back. As we merged onto the motorway we came close to hitting another car and in no way was it our fault, the stupid ass in the other car decided that he wanted to change lanes without letting anyone know that he wanted to do that. The box of cream cakes that had I bought earlier had sneakily appeared onto Jessica's lap and she had scoffed most of them by the time we arrived in the parking lot.

Planes were circling above us and Jessica yelled out. "Could one of these be her plane?" Just as she turned a ghostly white and threw up right down the front of my top.

"Oh god Sarah I'm so sorry!" She blurted out and then rummaged through her rather large mumsy bag to find a tissue. It was her first bout of morning sickness and it couldn't have chosen any other time start.

Everyone gathered around her to make sure she was ok, whilst I stood in the hot sun with the stench if vomit clinging to me. "What the fuck is it about me? Every time I meet up with Robbie something embarrassing happens to me. I stink, you guys. I can't go into the airport smelling like this."

Jessica began to convulse again from the smell that was omitting from my clothes but I couldn't handle it any longer myself and could feel my stomach turning over ready to join in with the puke fest.

"Sarah take your top off, you can wear my tee shirt for now." Charlie so graciously offered.

There I was in the middle of the car park stripping off my top in exchange for one that had a motive saying (Skirt Lifter). Grateful: Yes I was, embarrassed; totally.

Amongst all the commotion I caught sight of Jessica eyeing up Charlie's well formed muscles that had been built to perfection, and

Chapter Fourteen: Robbie's Back and She Brought Baggage

plus the fact that she wasn't wearing a bra left little to the imagination underneath her vest top.

We entered the waiting lounge and sat with all the other impatient people who were either clock watching or chasing after their energetic toddler children.

A large group of people that had been sitting in the row behind us had quietly disappeared and on one of the seats was an unattended brown suitcase. We waited for a few minutes for its owner to return before reporting it to customer services. The assistant immediately picked up the phone and the next thing we knew, were that trained officials came marching through the terminal stopping all would be travellers in their tracks and closing off the surrounding area. A bomb squad team were called in and as they were probing the bag with great caution, a naïve young man approached them and asked what they were doing to his luggage. Words were exchanged between them and then he was quickly escorted away from the area before normality was resumed. Then as the fluctuation of sun tanned people began to arrive, time stood still at the sight of Robbie entering the walk through. Goosebumps prickled all over my skin, my palms became sweaty and my legs turned to jelly. She was back, and my god was I ever happy.

I couldn't take my eyes off her as she hugged Kate with such delight. Apart from appearing a little weary from the long journey, she looked amazing and when it was my turn for a hug she shook my hand instead and thanked me for helping out with Kate then smiled sweetly.

Kate informed her that she had had a great time with me and our exciting adventures with our new friends, and she gave me a pat on the back as if to say, good job Sarah.

I picked up one of the cases from the trolley noticing that there were a couple of pink ones mixed in with them. Pink would definitely not be Robbie's colour choice.

"Ah yes." She said holding out her hand in the direction of a skinny young woman. "This is my friend Kiera."

We all exchanged introductions with each other, but Robbie was at an advantage as she had been informed of Charlie through Kate during their phone calls. I on the other hand was at a total loss as to who this Kiera was. She was of slim build with long blonde hair and immaculately dressed in a short skirt, low cut top and black heels. Almost a perfect reflection of how I would normally look. I brushed myself down and held my hand out to greet her just as a good will gesture, all the time feeling the urge to tear her hair right off from her head. I could feel the jealousy vibes rippling right through my veins as she gave a cold response and made it quite obvious in her mannerism that she wasn't going to be my friend at any cost. Apparently she had been friends with Robbie for years, but I could tell just by the false image she was portraying that I had a competition on my hands. That bitch was not going to step into my shoes and what kind of a name is Kiera anyway? The game was on, bring it bitch.

I knew that I looked like a desperate skank in my borrowed outfit and that I still smelt of Jessica's puke so at this point she had the upper hand right now, but this was just a temporary glitch.

"So you're Sarah the ex, nice shirt by the way." She remarked in such a high almighty manner.

Kate stepped in and suggested that we made a move. Right away this bitch handed me one of her cases to carry as if I was her fucking maid. Cheeky cow! But my good friend Charlie took charge and handed out a case for everyone to carry; even Kiera.

Robbie smiled at me and remarked on my physic which made me feel all goofy and tingly inside. My efforts in trying to cover up the logo on my top by crossing my arm over my chest and holding the case behind my shoulder lasted for five seconds. This was just one of those days in my life that I had to accept that my dignity had abandoned me.

We made our way through the terminal and as I walked on in front of Robbie, allowing her to catch up with the gossip from Kate, I could see her reflection in the glass panels as we past them, she was keeping a keen watch on my arse, so I made sure that she stayed in-

Chapter Fourteen: Robbie's Back and She Brought Baggage

terested by wiggling it even more, that is until Kiera caught on and distracted her attention. I was in the direct line of fire with no knowledge of this cow's background, and I needed to know just what exactly I was dealing with. One thing I knew for sure was that she was going to have a fight on her hands.

We got back to the car and we all stared at it like gormless morons trying to figure out how we were all going to fit inside with that entire luggage. Obviously Charlie and Kate sat in the front where Kate managed to squeeze two of the smaller cases down by her feet. Jessica sat by one of the doors and put a bag on the floor so that she could rest her feet on it, and bloody Kiera volunteered to sit on Robbie's lap by the other door because she apparently got car sick and needed to be by the window, which left me sandwiched in the middle with one bag on my lap and another under my feet. The rest of the luggage was crammed into the boot with minimal space to spare.

Charlie opened the window a little as she could see that I was getting overheated and flustered. I was never any good in confined spaces and could feel myself freaking out inside. Most of the conversation went back and forth between Robbie and Kate with constant interruptions from Kiera. I wanted to explode on her; this whole situation had become a farce. What the hell was I thinking meeting Robbie at the airport? She didn't want me there she had other plans on her mind and I had unknowingly interfered with them. We were all feeling a little uncomfortable and I felt it was entirely my fault.

As soon as we got back to Kate's we unloaded the car and I nudged Charlie's arm and mouthed to her to get me the fuck out of here. She immediately responded to my request and made an excuse that she had to leave and would drop me and Jessica off on the way. We said our goodbyes and I informed Kate that I would be over for a chat soon. That's when I heard Kiera mutter; not too soon I hope. Was it me or was everyone else oblivious to her rudeness? Robbie's eyes were fixated on me as she whispered to Kiera to behave herself and be nicer to me but I couldn't get in the car soon enough and once we were out of their sight I let out an almighty scream from my built up frustration. Charlie and Jessica joined in with me until our throats couldn't hold the sound anymore.

Charlie told me that I had handled the situation with the up most dignity, especially from that snotty cow.

"Sarah we still love you." Jessica kindly pointed out obviously understanding how pissed off I was right now.

"I know, you guys are really good friends to me and I'm lucky to have you in my life right now." Was Jessica actually referring to the fact that she and Charlie were now we?

Charlie looked at me in the rear view mirror and said; "You're gonna be just fine babe, you're a fighter. That bitch will never prove herself to Robbie, you mark my words."

"I'm sure you're right Charlie, somehow I feel like I'm just falling apart all over again and I need to gain control back in my life; starting with a fresh set of clothes."

My desperation for Robbie was crushing me and I didn't want her to compare my likeness to Jens; as a stalker, so for now I just had to ride the wave.

"Hey girl I think we're gonna treat you to a beer, are you up for it?" Charlie asked and then whispered say yes, say yes.

I wasn't sure how I was feeling and maybe drinking wasn't the answer but my decline went unheard as Jessica pleaded with me to go. She tormented me with a special club she'd been to with Jen. God knows why I accepted, but I did.

We went back to mine so that I could shower and change into something sexy, and Charlie cooked a pizza and cracked open a couple of beers for us. I emerged from my room looking so hot that Jessica even commented that I could get any chick I wanted. My sexy shell only held deep sadness on the inside, but putting on a show was something that I was good at.

Charlie and I downed a few beers before scoffing the rest of the pizza and I was already beginning to feel a little light headed.

We arrived by cab outside a small clubhouse where there was a black door with a staircase directly behind it. Everyone was dressed

Chapter Fourteen: Robbie's Back and She Brought Baggage

in black and the music was at a low volume which I thought to be unusual. We ordered drinks from the bar and sat at a table next to a large black curtain which was hanging across an entrance way to another room. A woman stood at the side taking money as people entered and I could hear a regular occurrence of clapping. I looked at Charlie and Jessica and asked them why people were applauding when there were no sounds of cheers or entertainment. Jessica almost choked on her drink and then burst out laughing.

"Come on." She said grabbing my hand and almost dragging me off my seat. "Let's go in so you can see what's really going on."

She showed the woman a membership card and paid ten pounds for each of us to go inside. As we pulled the curtain across and entered I saw men and women tied up in leather restraints by their wrists and ankles and most of them were fully naked proudly showing off their sinful shows of being whipped and degraded in front of an audience of silent enthusiasts. The clapping sound I had heard was coming from a woman dressed in a black PVC corset and shorts standing over a young female who had been straddled faced downward on a small wooden structure that looked as though it had been specially made for this purpose. She was slapping her naked arse cheeks with what looked like a small black leather paddle. A crowd had gathered round to watch and I could see that they were all clearly getting off from it; even I began to feel drawn to the sleazy excitement.

My mind began to wonder at the thought of whether Jen had brought Robbie here to enjoy the controlled sadistic torture. Had they put on a show for these strangers? It was disturbing to think that someone I cared for so deeply could possibly have resorted to giving her dignity away in this form, but Kate had mentioned that Robbie did have a dark side maybe this is what she meant.

Jessica nudged me and asked if I'd had enough of the scenery. I nodded yes as I took a large swig of my beer. We went back into the other room and I saw Charlie brush her hand down Jessica's arm in a slow gliding sensual manner. Her charisma must have been working as Jessica didn't flinch at the thought of it. I leaned in towards her and whispered in her ear that it was ok to go for it, I could see that there was a connection between them and that I was totally fine with it.

Jessica was reluctant to admit anything at first but then she confided with me that she had feelings for Charlie but was worried that it was just her hormones playing tricks on her. I assured her that if she felt this way she should act on it as I knew Charlie was just bursting to tell her that she had fallen for her.

"I kind of had the feeling that she liked me. Sarah do you mind if I… oh never mind I'm just gonna do it."

She grabbed Charlie by the hand and pulled her close, so close that when their lips met Jessica went the whole hog and planted a wet sloppy kiss right on Charlie's mouth.

I slowly stepped away in the direction of the bar and got myself another beer. As I waited I watched the two of them combine their worlds into one immaculate sensual act of kissing. Had Charlie finally found her soul mate and had Jessica finally found someone who would love her back in the way that she deserved.

"Here's to new beginnings." I toasted aloud to myself.

CHAPTER FIFTEEN
SWING LOW LITTLE SISTER

We finished the night off with me getting absolutely plastered and when the cab driver dropped me off first, Charlie had to carry me to my front door. I gave both of them a big kiss and told them how much I loved them. Then standing on my doorstep I waved as hard as I could as they drove away. Then I made a helpless effort to put the key in the lock and constantly missed the target each time I made the approach. That's when I noticed the gate to the next door neighbour's garden was open. A child's swing caught my attention so I felt compelled to go over and sit on it; just for a moment. I started swinging slowly and then did the stupidest thing ever. I twisted the swing in a circular movement making the ropes tangle together; only I was unaware that my hair was also being entwined in the spin and being pulled upwards with the ropes. The pull became so tight that it felt like I had just had a face lift. I couldn't free myself from the twisted mass and at first I thought it was quite funny and I began to laugh. But when I realised that I was freaking stuck, the seriousness of it began to sink in. My bag was on the ground with my phone inside and I couldn't get it with my foot. Each time I moved to try to drag it, my hair pulled tighter. What the fuck was I to do?

"Can somebody help me?" I yelled. "Help, can anybody hear me? Please help me." And now another of my stupid decisions had put me into a dilemma and I wondered how long it was going to take before I got somebody's attention.

A figure emerged from the gateway of the garden but I could only see their silhouette as the street light was behind them.

"Help me please, my hair is caught in these ropes and I'm in pain when I move. I'm stuck here." I was so embarrassed but at the same time totally relieved that someone was coming to save me.

The person came closer and then I noticed that it was a woman coming to my rescue. That woman then turned out to be Robbie. Her soft voice calmed me as she sussed the situation out and tried to figure out what she was going to do to help set me free.

"Sarah what are you doing here?" She asked inquisitively.

Her hands were gentle as she tried to loosen my strands from the ropes and the tears began to roll down my cheeks as I felt extremely humble towards her. I breathed in her fragrance of citrusy notes as she stood in front of me and I so desperately wanted to wrap my arms around her waist and hold her tightly never to let her kind sole leave me again.

"I thought it would be fun." I sobbed. "I had no idea that this god awful thing was going to keep me as its prisoner." My mascara began to run down my face causing my eyes to sting but I was more concerned about trying not to stain her clothing right now.

"Never mind you're in safe hands now." She said gently untangling my locks taking great care not to cause me any more pain.

As she managed to set me free in less than twenty minutes she reassured me that I was going to be medically fine then scooped me up in her arms and carried me back to the safety of my apartment where she sat me down on the sofa and poured me a large glass of water. I really needed something a little stronger but I knew that would have been a huge mistake.

"I feel such a fool Robbie and I don't know why I did that but it was lucky that you came along when you did. You're my hero you know. Why are you here anyway?" It hadn't occurred to me that she had just appeared at the right moment.

"Well I wanted to see you to thank you in person. It was a little strange at the airport, I could feel the uneasy atmosphere between everyone and I know that you have been a big help to Kate and to me as well, you're my hero too."

"Thank you; I appreciate your acknowledgment on my new super skills. I've had a lot of fun with Kate and I hope that I can continue to do so, if that's alright with you?" She was now one of my many new best friends and I didn't want to lose that.

Chapter Fifteen: Swing Low Little Sister

My eagerness to please Robbie was itching to explode but I knew that I had to play the role of the martyr and be patient with her and I could see that she wanted to say more to me but something was preventing her.

"Sarah, Kiera is just a friend I want you to know that. I've known her since I was five years old and she has been a rock to me when I've needed stability in my life; she just needed a holiday and kind of invited herself along. Her role in my life is purely innocent." Her eyes were like watery pools of blue Safire and I wanted to kiss her full red lips, as in my mind they would taste of the finest sensual essence I could ever wish to experience.

"Robbie I've missed you so much!" I blurted out then slapped my hand over my mouth to stop any more words from foolishly leaving my lips.

"I've missed you too Sarah, and if I've hurt you, well I just want to say I'm sorry. I'm sorry for completely misjudging you and assuming that you were just like all the others in my past."

I could feel myself longing to hold her, to put everything on the line and to hell with the consequences. "Oh Robbie I've been a lost cause without you. I'm not sure who I am anymore."

"You'll be fine Sarah; you've changed a lot in the past few months. My girl has grown up." She said as she stroked my hair away from my cheek.

"And I'm sorry about your mother; I never really got a chance to say anything to you earlier."

She patted my knee and gave me a sympathetic look but I could see sadness enveloping her as the thought of losing her mother was beginning to sink in.

"My mother was more like a friend to me, she was great and I miss her tremendously. My brother and sister can't wait to get their hands on the money from the sale of the house. I despise them so much for that and they were the reason for my early return."

She began to explain to me the history of her family background and how her brother and sister turned their backs on her when she came out. And that her mother accepted her lifestyle and even had in depth conversations about her current girlfriends. They had maintained a close relationship as mother and daughter and Robbie had always listened to her advice even if she didn't use it.

We had a light hearted conversation about when I introduced Charlie to my parents at Christmas and how worried I was about telling them and how relieved I was to find that they too accepted it quite easily. It was getting extremely late and my tiredness began to take its toll on my body. I yawned several times during our conversation trying hard to keep it from happening.

"I'm sorry Robbie that's so rude of me; it's been a long day."

"Sure I had better make a move Kiera will be wondering where I've got to." She got up to leave but I felt the need to stop her in her tracks.

"Why don't you stay?" I shrilled like an excited teenager. "It's late and not safe to be out on your own at this time of night."

"No Sarah I couldn't, I have to get back." She was determined to leave but I wanted more of her.

"Please Robbie, it's so lonely being me these days, your company would be so refreshing. Please, I'm begging you." I gave her a sad puppy expression so that she would feel sorry for me. That seemed to do the trick quite nicely. Not that I was being sneaky or anything.

"Oh Sarah what is it about you that I can't say no to." I knew from the way that she smiled that she was glad to be staying over.

The tiredness that had empowered me suddenly left leaving me with a surge of energy so I jumped up immediately and grabbed two beers from the fridge and plonked them down in front of her on the coffee table.

"I'll be back in just a sec. Just gonna get changed into something more comfortable."

Practically running to the bedroom I chose to put on a long tee shirt that just covered my arse and also revealed my nipples allowing them to protrude and a black lacy thong finished off the sexy look I was going for. I was only gone momentarily and quick stepped it back to join her on the sofa.

"Are you enjoying your beer? I have others if you're not." I felt awkward at not knowing what to say to her and found myself twiddling my hair into ringlets as my nerves were beginning to take over. "Would you like crisps? Or I have crackers and cheese." Or me I thought? Oh god crisps, crackers, cheese, what was I thinking? Quick think of something intelligent to say, I'm gonna bore her to death and she'll soon be reminded of why she left me.

"So I have a feeling that Kiera doesn't like me, but that's ok she doesn't really know me, not like you and Kate do."

"I don't think it's like that Sarah, she's just looking out for me, but I'll have a word with her if she's making you feel uncomfortable. I would like us all to be friends. She really has no need to have a problem with you, and everything I told her about you was all positive. I haven't bad mouthed you at all I promise." I could see her glancing at my body every now and again and I knew that I was starting to win her over.

"Are we just friends Robbie?" I asked as I snuggled my head into her shoulder.

"Yes Sarah we are." She wrapped her arm around me sending a tingle of arousal right through my body.

I closed my eyes and lightly mouthed the words, I love you, not knowing whether she heard me but at least my feelings were out there now. We sipped our beers as we reacquainted with each other until 3am. That was when I suggested that we carry on our conversation in my bed. Just in case we should happen to fall asleep I pointed out.

We lay on top of the duvet facing each other and holding hands. I watched her eyes with intense fascination as my mind raced with thoughts of; touch me, kiss me now.

She had removed most of her clothing apart from a tee shirt and a pair of her favourite boxer shorts and I was desperate to feel her rippling muscles that were just calling out for my hands to wonder over them. The temptation was teasing me to the point of torture and I had to know how she felt about me.

I stroked my hand down her arm and put the words out there. "Robbie, how do you feel about me?"

"I'm very fond of you and I think you're a wonderful person. You were kind enough to put your life on hold to help out with Kate at such short notice and I really appreciate that."

I had expected a more intimate response than that but then my reality check kicked in and made me realise that I wasn't going to get the information that I wanted to hear. Not yet anyway.

The daylight started to seep through the gap in the curtains and our tiredness took its toll on us. We fell asleep around 5.30 am and my dreams were sweet as I slept peacefully into the morning.

CHAPTER SIXTEEN

PINK HEARTS AND A NEW MAKEOVER

*I*t turned out that I had slept heavily until noon, so heavily that I hadn't heard Robbie get up and leave. She had written me a short note and put it on my pillow for me to find when I awoke. The note read: "Thanks for a relaxed evening. Sorry I had to leave before you woke up and I promise that we will have an exciting night together soon just the two of us. Keep wearing that beautiful smile that I love. Robbie X."

My spirits were lifted as I felt a glimmer of hope that there might possibly be something between us after all. My tangled feelings of lust and love had grown stronger than ever and I just prayed that she felt the same way towards me. I had to share my exciting news with Jessica so I called her immediately.

"Hi it's me, your local idiot."

"Hey babe what's up?" She replied, not dismissing my claim to stupidity.

"Well I thought I should tell you that I got stuck on a swing last night and my hair got tangled. This all happened after you guys dropped me off."

"What do you mean? I mean how did you? I mean, I don't know what I mean." She stammered her words whilst still trying to process how this could have happened.

"Well I went into the neighbour's garden and my hair got caught up in the ropes as I spun round in a circle, you know, the sort of thing we did as kids. But that's not the end of it. Guess who came to my rescue?" I knew she wouldn't be able to guess she was never any good at that game.

"Oh my god who was it?" She squealed in excitement.

"Robbie! She heard my cries of help. She was on her way over to see me, so that she could talk to me alone to thank me properly. Jessica she ended up staying the night! I think there might be a chance for us to reconcile after all." I could feel the joy returning back into my life just at the mere prospect that there might be a possibility she would want me once again.

"So you two are back on then. Did you get intimate, was it better than before? Come on give me some details." She was just as excited as I was at my news.

I wished that I had more to tell her but the time wasn't right yet. "Not quite yet, but I don't think it will be long before we are. Oh god Jessica I can't believe she's back." I could hear Charlie talking in the background and I asked Jessica how things were with the two of them.

"Oh Sarah she's wonderful. She also spent the night but we did more than just sleep if you know what I mean." I knew exactly what she was saying the dirty cow.

"So you two fucked?" Maybe pregnancy did have its advantages after all.

"Oh yeah, but she was so gentle and caring about my needs. At first I was so conscious of my bump but she put me right at ease and made me feel that I was special. Are you ok hearing this? I don't want to upset you if you still have any feelings for her."

"God no, we're just good mates now. You're the one I have concerns for and you have a bump already?"

She whispered into the phone that she came twice within minutes and that no one had ever done that to her before, not even Jen possessed the powers that be to do that. Sarah if this is what love and passion is all about then I want this forever." Her voice sounded full of vibrant sparkle as she filled me in with the intimate details of her love making, and I had a feeling that Charlie was going to be faithful with Jessica as she wouldn't be the sort of person to crap all over a pregnant woman's emotions.

"I'm pleased for you both, but you do have to get things sorted out with Jake. He is an unpredictable sleazebag, but as the father of your child he will have legal rights. Be careful Jessica, that's all I'm saying." I had a nagging feeling that he wasn't going to leave as gracefully as she was hoping for and that she was going to be in for quite a bumpy ride.

"I do understand where you're coming from Sarah, and I agree with you, he is scum, that's why I don't want him in my life any more, or the baby's for that matter." Yep definitely not seeing this from the point of reality is she.

"Ok well the way I see it is that you don't have to have any dealings with him until the baby is born, so you do have time to set down some ground rules. Maybe you should handle everything through a solicitor and keep your stress levels down."

"I know babe, and if Charlie has her way I'll be getting plenty of rest. Anyway let's get back to you and Robbie in the house of love." I liked the sound of that.

I explained about the note and that I was ecstatically happy that things had happened between us emotionally, and how I looked forward to our next rendezvous.

"Well girl I think that might be an excuse for us to go girlie shopping. Get your arse over here; I'm sure Charlie can give you some good advice on what would turn Robbie's attention once and for all." That was the first sensible thing she had said today.

"Ok then I'd like that. I'll be over shortly. Bye." Maybe it was time to improve my image although I found it hard to improve on perfection once perfection had been reached, and that was exactly what I was looking at in the mirror.

We ended up going into several stores including my own, where I tried on different types of jeans and skirts. Charlie advised me on a hot pair of jeans with leather pockets on the back. They gave my ass a heart shape appearance, they were a definite purchase. I matched them up with a sleeveless black tee shirt that showed my arms off well, my workouts had paid off. A leather belt with a large pewter buckle and an embossed cross gave a masculine look to the set up, but still that touch of femininity.

"Now all you need are a great pair of boots and you're done." Jessica implied as she spun me around to check that every curve was being shown to its fullest potential.

Charlie knew the exact place to go as boots were her forte. My look was complete and my part in the dyke world was becoming clearer as the meaning of my journey began to make more sense.

As we walked out of the store Jessica made a suggestion that I would look good with a tattoo and that there was a tattooist just across the street. I was a big chicken when it came to needles so it was a great surprise to find myself saying yes to the idea. As we entered the huge glass doorway that span the entire front of the store we were greeted by a young girl with long black hair tied up in a pony tail allowing her neck and shoulders to show colourful visions of cherry blossoms and orchids. She presented us with an album full of different pictures and portraits but I wanted simplicity with meaning. So I chose to go with a pink heart to go on the back of my neck. It meant to me that I had been kissed there by a beautiful woman and I wanted the memory of it to stay with me forever.

The tattoo artist understood how nervous I was so he put on a DVD for us all to watch whilst he got on with his artwork. The film began and then I felt this tremendous surge of scratching at my skin which immediately threw me into a major sweat fest. What seemed like an eternity lasted for twenty minutes before the announcement; "I'm done, would you like to take a look?" He had used a deep pink ink that really showed well against my skin tone and as simple as it was I felt like I had just had the most amazing tattoo that anybody could ever have chosen.

I had to wear a patch over it for a few hours but once I was able to show it off I felt a little special having done something so different to myself.

We went back to Charlie's place and I gained the approval from Jez and Jules and at the suggestion that my hair needed a makeover they were on the case, and before I knew it I had blonde highlights and burgundy lowlights on my under layers.

Chapter Sixteen: Pink Hearts and A New Makeover

"Oh girl she had better love this look." Jessica announced proudly as she flicked and played around with my locks.

Charlie held my hand and said that any woman would be a fool not to fall for me. My new look was impressive and I now had a powerful image with a touch of innocence. I loved everything about my new makeover.

We celebrated my new sensational style by going clubbing and Charlie was right; I pulled several times that night. I was very flattered by the whole idea of being every woman's fantasy, but my goal was set and I wasn't about to fuck up any more. My confidence had been re-established and the hunt was on, and I had become the hunter.

Jessica had arranged that we would go round to Kate's in the morning, giving me the excuse to show off my fit assets, so I kept my drinking to a minimal. Then we all danced the night away and it felt strange to stay sober when the others were getting completely wrecked around me.

The next morning couldn't have come soon enough; I put the straighteners through my hair creating a glossy sexy look and slipped into my new gear. My make up was kept to a light natural look giving me a fresh youthful glow.

We arrived at Kate's in no time and standing outside her door Jessica reassured me on how hot I looked. "Now Sarah, keep your composure and make sure you calm down a little with that smile. You don't want to scare the woman off do you?" She giggled.

"Oh god I'm making a twat out of myself before I even see her. Jessica I'm acting like an idiot, let's go before I make a huge mistake." This was not a good time to have a meltdown; again I found myself making stupid decisions that could have reverse consequences.

"It's ok Sarah, just focus, now breathe slowly and brace yourself." She began to breathe slowly herself showing me that I too should join in.

At that comment she knocked on the door and rang the bell at the same time, making sure our arrival was heard by all.

I smoothed my shirt down over the top of my jeans and when I looked up expecting to be greeted by a friendly host we found ourselves being faced by no other than bloody Kiera. I had temporarily forgotten about this nemesis.

She stood there, put her hand to her mouth and let out a loud laugh before making a spiteful comment. "What the hell have you done to yourself? You look so left behind in the 90's."

I could have slapped her right there. Who the fuck did she think she was.

"Hi Kiera we've come to see Kate." Jessica politely informed her.

"Yes come in quickly, I don't want you embarrassing me anymore in front of the neighbours. Come on hurry." Bitch was too good of a word for her right now.

My fists were clenched as I barged past her in the hallway, just one punch from me and she would have been out for a week, but that wasn't on the agenda, not today anyway but definitely on my; I owe you list.

"Is that you Sarah?" I heard Kate call from the lounge.

"Yes Kate, I'm here with Jessica."

Upon entering the lounge I saw Kate sitting on the sofa with Robbie at her side. They were entering data onto her laptop and it seemed that they were quite grateful for the interruption as they hadn't taken a break from it all morning.

"Well hello there ladies." Kate said with an inviting smile on her face.

I bent down and gave her a kiss on each cheek before coolly acknowledging Robbie with a smile and a stupid half wave. She in return acknowledged me back with a warm smile of her own and our eyes met and stayed focused for what seemed like ages. Then there was a rude interruption of coughing followed by a cackling voice. "Can I get either of you a drink?"

I refused to even look at that bitch and pretended that she wasn't there. No one else existed in that room and I kept my eyes fixated on Robbie's as I sat in the arm chair.

Chapter Sixteen: Pink Hearts and A New Makeover

Robbie suggested that we go and sit out in the garden while Kate and Jessica discussed business and as she stood up she reached out for my hand and I quickly latched on to her letting her guide me through the kitchen and out onto the patio area of the garden. The sun was shining down through the branches of the trees and the fragrance of the French lavenders filled the air as a light breeze carried a welcomed feel of freshness.

We had only sat down for a moment when we were joined by the sound of clinking glasses. The sight of Kiera carrying a tray of cold drinks and approaching us gave the whole idea of romance a bad smell. Given the choice I would rather be faced with the turd from an elephant than have to look at her rat face features.

"I thought you might want something cold to drink in this heat so I made a cocktail of orange juice, blackcurrant and a hit of vodka. Hope you like it ladies!"

Thoughts in my head were screaming, why don't you just fuck off? Then I realised that she could quite easily resurrect the bitch inside me that I once was. She immediately made herself comfortable by sitting at the table with us and started making comments about how long she had known Robbie and then made comparisons to me and other girls from Robbie's past. She was trying to piss on her turf as tho Robbie belonged to her like a possession. I kept reminding myself not to rise to her pathetic level, not in front of Robbie anyway. This cow seemed to love herself too much and if she thought that she was going to win Robbie over me then she was going to get a bigger fight than she expected.

"Hey Sarah nice tattoo by the way, I really like the pink on you."

"Thanks Robbie I got it yesterday. It hurt like hell for a short while but I'm glad I've done it now. I'm glad you like it though." It's where you kissed me, it's where you kissed me, I sang silently to myself.

Kiera belted out that she had a tattoo of a butterfly on her boob. She got it just after Robbie had hers. She then proceeded to reach inside her top and remove the ghastly object known as a tit from her bra and pushed it right into Robbie's face. It was a completely cheap act that gained no pay off from the recipient. Robbie just smiled and politely said that it was a nice tattoo then turned her attentions back to me. There was a glorious silent ringing of bells going on inside my head as I had clearly won that round.

Robbie stroked her finger across the back of my hand and we talked about how nice it was going to be having Jessica living in the house, especially when the baby is born.

I happily volunteered to help move her in and decorate the baby's room. Kiera boasted how good she was at home décor and deciding where things should be placed. Probably more like giving out orders in the form of a bossy cow. I liked the way that Robbie humoured her by pretending to pay attention to what she was saying but not being overly impressed with her comments. She even apologised to me in front of Kiera for her poor mannerism towards me, but Kiera pretended not to notice that she was offending me. I felt irritated inside but was more than determined to not let her see this.

We were soon joined by Jessica and Kate, who were very happy to announce that Jessica was going to move in this weekend coming. We toasted our drinks to the new merger and conversation after that revolved around Jessica and her new adventures to come. She was going to rent the entire upstairs which was more than ample space for one grown up and a little baby.

When it was time to leave, there were lots of hugs and kisses between Kate and Jessica and offers of supplying snacks for everyone on moving day.

Robbie invited herself back to my place which gave me great joy. We decided to walk and our pace was slow due to the fact that Jessica wasn't able to sprint. I was on cloud nine as Robbie held my hand all the way back, showing me off proudly to the world like her prized possession. We left Jessica at the end of her street before returning to my palace of chaos.

The apartment was a complete mess, my clothes were once again scattered everywhere and there were dirty glasses and plates on the table.

Chapter Sixteen: Pink Hearts and A New Makeover

"Oh Sarah it's just like the first day I walked in here." She laughed as she prodded at a pair of shoes I had left hanging by their straps on the back of a chair.

"Shit I didn't expect you to come back here." I remarked fully embarrassed, I would have tidied up if I'd known any better.

Then she made her move on me by running her fingers through my hair and then guided my head gently to a slight angle positioning me for a romantic kiss. I just froze on the spot. Could this really be happening to me? Were we really going to be an item again?

She pressed her lips against mine and I allowed my mouth to follow the sensual instructions that it was being given. I pressed harder into the kiss as I received her intense greeting. Then she began to lightly nibble and kiss my neck as her hands performed the act of undoing my bra beneath my top prompting me to lift my arms in the air to allow her to remove my tee shirt swiftly. Her warm wet tongue tickled my nipples making them erect and the intensity of the pleasure was turning me on immensely. Taking hold of my hands she slowly pulled me to the bedroom where she took complete control of removing the rest of my garments. Using her foot to part my legs slightly for better access she placed her hand inside my knickers and inserted her fingers into me starting with short light enjoyable thrusts, whilst paying extreme attention to my responsive enthusiasm the entire time. This woman had aroused my entire body with such great force that I was now at the point of need. I was responding freely; waiting for her next move; waiting to show her how sophisticated my bedroom antics had become so I lay down on the bed with my inviting body waiting patiently, watching her performance as she undressed herself. She moved in on top of me; the muscles in her arms were pumped to their fullest as she supported her weight. Then she began to kiss my ribcage, slowly gliding her tongue downwards causing me to writhe up and down indulgently, wanting her, needing her, not caring at this point what she was going to do to me, just to bloody well do it. My excitement was at its highest when her hands parted my inner thighs open; my breathing became deep and heavy and I tilted my head back as her tongue pressed its way onto my clitoris with gentle twisting strokes that became more intense as she strived for my complete submission. My orgasm was surprisingly reached within minutes before she finished off the sexual activity by kissing my inner thighs then my stomach followed by consecutive kisses to my breasts before moving back up to face level with me. Tears of joy rolled down my face as not so long ago I thought that this moment was never going to happen again.

"What's wrong Sarah, didn't you enjoy it?" Using the edge of the bed sheet she lightly wiped away the wet residue that had formed beneath my eyes then planted a sweet kiss on each of them.

"Oh my god yes I did." I sobbed. "I love you, I love you Robbie so much that it hurts my heart."

"I love you too Sarah. I've loved you from the moment I first met you but I had to be sure that you felt the same way about me. I was just too scared to let go of my feelings and open up to you only to find that you'd turn out to be another Jen." I completely understood where she was coming from with that.

"Robbie, promise me you won't ever leave me again; promise me." My sobbing was uncontrollable as she put her arms around me and comforted me with her warmth and tenderness.

"I promise baby." She whispered into my ear. "I'll never leave my girl again."

I held on tightly to her body not wanting to let her go and then the words came from her mouth that I had longed to hear. "Make love to me Sarah Niles Page."

The sound of my new name sent tingles shooting down my spine and I couldn't believe that she was ready for me to reveal my insatiate talents on her. My nerves were showing as I wanted to be the one who made her feel that her entire life had been missing the most important piece of the puzzle. No pressure there I thought.

I began by kissing her breasts slowly; all the time conscious of my actions and watching her face for signs of approval. I moved downwards, maybe a little too hastily, I wasn't too sure, and then I tasted

Chapter Sixteen: Pink Hearts and A New Makeover

her. It was an awkward moment but I overcame it quite quickly; stopping to make sure that I was giving it to her in the proper manner that it should be received; she pushed my head back down with the answer uh huh. Her breathing became heavier and she lifted her buttocks up into the air and grabbed my hair hard as she made the announcement that she was cumming. I had managed to bring her to orgasm, an achievement that I was quite proud of. Planting slow sensual kisses to every curve of her body; teasing her senses as I did; I worked my way back up to her irresistible lips greeting them with a passion so intensified that she became submissive to my power.

She looked into my eyes and straight away I felt her emotional contentment, her desire had been fully satisfied; her smile was radiant and her body was spent.

"Sarah I want to make you happy. I have dreamt of this moment for such a long time, you have completed me, and my affection for you is so insanely strong."

I embraced every word she spoke and with a feeling of blissful sexual satisfaction we drifted off to sleep holding each other tightly.

The next morning I awoke to the smell of pancakes cooking. I got up quickly and went to the kitchen where I was greeted by my wife who was dressed only in a grey tee shirt.

"Good morning my little ray of sunshine." She said as she held her arms out to greet me.

"Hey you're cooking my favourite yummy food." My appetite was huge this morning and I couldn't wait to scoff them down.

We hugged each other to the sound of spattering batter; to me, it was all so romantic. Our breakfast time was spent with lots of giggles and happy smiles at the knowledge of having been engaged in divaliscious sex play.

"You are moving back in aren't you? I mean this is for real." I had to hear the confirmation come from her lips just to be sure that I wasn't assuming that things were going to happen.

"Sarah will you stop rambling. We are solid, I love you! Ok! And yes I'll move back in." She fed me another piece of pancake from her plate and some of the butter dripped down my chin but that was a good accident as she got up and kissed it off for me.

"I'm sorry Robbie; I just still can't believe you're here with me that's all and what about Kiera? What's going to happen to her?" Maybe she could just disappear from our lives for good never to return.

After a brief moment I made a difficult decision that would probably bite me in the ass, but I needed Robbie to see that I would do anything for her, so I offered to allow Kiera to stay with us, you know keep your enemies close.

"Maybe she could stay in your old room. I really don't mind. We can call her after breakfast if you like and tell her our news." Oh god say no please say no it's a terrible idea but thank you any way.

"Are you sure Sarah? I know you're not too keen on the way that she portrays herself. But I'm sure she'll behave herself once she sees how much we mean to each other." The devil himself wasn't gonna get the chance to break our new found bond so what chance did she have?

"Tell you what we'll set some ground rules. If she keeps up with this facade then she can leave. Is that ok with you?" I remarked. Chances are she won't last a day if I have anything to do with it.

"You come first with me Sarah; now speaking of coming, get in that bedroom, or do you want to be ravaged here on the table?" There was a mischievous glint in her eye and I knew I was in for some sinful fun.

She jumped up swiftly and chased me around the kitchen screaming with laughter before capturing and pinning me to the ground. Good job she's a clean freak I thought. My breathing became heavy as she took control and I grabbed hold of the table leg as she once again teased my body into a frenzied hot wet throbbing sensation.

By that afternoon Kiera had sent all of her cases and belongings over; courtesy of a taxi cab, not giving one thought to include any of Robbie's gear, so Charlie came to our rescue and went with Robbie to help pack up her belongings and transport them over, whilst I remained behind and made room in our closet for the extra clothing it was about to be filled with. Kiera the lazy bitch just dumped her stuff on the lounge floor and sat on the sofa drinking a glass of wine that she had helped herself to out of my fucking fridge.

"There's something you should know Sarah." She yelled out. "I like to take long showers and only drink expensive bottled water. So if you don't have any in can you make sure to get some next time you're out, thanks?" Because it would be too much trouble for you to move wouldn't it.

"Fuck you!" I muttered under my breath.

"Oh and if you're doing any ironing I've got a few things that need to be pressed and hung up." I had a feeling that she was going to be waiting rather a long time for any of her gear to look fresh.

I totally blanked her out as she just wasn't worth the effort at that point and when Robbie and Charlie arrived back I directed them straight into the bedroom.

"Kiera you haven't moved your cases into your room yet." She shot up quickly out of the chair startled by Robbie's comment.

"Oh I know Robbie I'm just about to now. I was actually waiting for you to come back first, you know, so we could have some girlie fun while you chatted to me as I put my stuff away. That's what we're going to do isn't it?" Wow! Had I just stepped onto planet Kiera?

Robbie just looked at me and mouthed I'm sorry but I put on a brave face and made out that I was ok with it. I could see that things were going to be fun around here for a while.

I thanked Charlie for being such a big help to us and we were both entirely grateful to have such a good friend. I was glad to see that she and Robbie had accepted each other's friendship quite easily as well. Charlie said her goodbyes and we arranged to meet up on Saturday to help with the big move for Jessica.

The next couple of days were spent easily with me going off to work and Robbie off to Kate's, leaving Kiera at home on her own to do what she was best at; absolutely nothing. We would finish each day by cleaning up the mess that she had created and even cooked her meals, as we were afraid of what crap she would leave us to deal with. After asking her what she had been up to all day she replied that she had been bored stiff, that this country was so dull, or that she had slept most of the day. I thought that I was lazy but she took the trophy for that one.

On the day of Jessica's move Charlie packed her car full with as many items as possible and the moving company dealt with all the larger items. The three of us got stuck in with the hard labour whilst Jessica and Kate decided what would look nice where. The wonderful Kiera was nowhere in sight of course. In fact she hadn't even emerged from her room that morning, not that I cared too much, but at least it gave me a break from her tiring sarcasm. We spent most of the day going up and down stairs carrying boxes of Jessica's personal possessions and when the last one was off loaded we all enjoyed a takeout meal, Jessica's treat of course. When we were just about to tuck in to our well deserved food Kiera decided to grace us with her ferret face.

"God I'm so tired." She moaned as she approached us. "Umm food d'you mind, I couldn't be bothered to cook anything."

"Are you fucking kidding me?" I snapped at her. "We've been breaking our backs all day while you slept."

She picked at the foil trays of food, tasting everything on offer, double dipping as well the shallow cow.

"Oh well it takes a lot of energy to be me. Besides you guys look like you can handle this shit on your own." It was hard to not to think that she was one smart cookie but her attitude towards me and my friends was absolutely disgraceful.

Robbie stood up to her and calmly informed her that if she was going to be a guest under our roof, she had better start showing a little more respect towards me and our friends, and to stop causing so much lesbian disturbia but it just fell on deaf ears.

"Oh yeah by the way Robs, you'll never guess who I bumped into on the way over here? Your ex girlfriend; that sexy vixen, Jen. Oh and she said to say hi to you Sarah, actually what she really said was, tell my little fuck freak hi. We had a really interesting conversation about you." Now she too was privy to my most intimate dealings with that stalker; was there anybody in London that didn't know?

My first reaction was to check for reassurance from Robbie that things were cool between us, as I know that if the shoe had been on the other foot I would have been having a hysterical hissy fit.

Kate interrupted Kiera during her triumphant moment of glory in the; I scored full marks in the; I'll get you bitch competition. "Kiera eat some more food, there's plenty for us all." She offered picking up a tray of chicken chow main and placing it into Kiera's hands.

"Thank you Kate I think I will. So Sarah how long did you and Jen fuck each other's brains out for?" I watched her pop a noodle into her gob and hoped that it would get stuck and choke her to death.

I couldn't keep my temper in any longer and clenching my fists tightly I began screaming at her. "That's it I'm not taking anymore shit from you Kiera. I've put up with so much of your crap infested mouth for Robbie's sake, but now you can just fuck right off."

At this point Robbie stepped in and informed Kiera that it was time for her to leave. She told her that their friendship had come to an insufferable end because they had turned into total strangers.

"You've been an absolute bitch to me since we met." I happily added into the conversation.

Kiera pleaded with Robbie not to throw her out and she tried to justify why she had been so awful to me. Her jealousy of my relationship with Robbie had affected her behaviour. She knew that I was the one that Robbie loved and she found it hard to deal with. She had always waited for a weak moment in Robbie's life just so that she could jump at the chance to gain enough trust from her that their friendship would turn into a sexual one. She had been in love with Robbie for years and hated seeing how well she treated me compared to her past girlfriends.

Robbie was shocked at this revelation and told Kiera that there could never be anything beyond what they already had.

I felt proud that my girl was sticking up for me and with the adrenaline rushing through my veins I wanted Robbie to really stick it to her.

Charlie and Jessica sat in silence during the whole episode probably feeling a little awkward. Kate tried to keep things calm between us all. Kiera started sniffling and her eyes were filled with tears, crocodile tears if anything, she even promised Robbie that she would behave herself if she could stay. Funny how I never heard the words sorry leave her sour lips.

"I think that's up to Sarah to decide." Robbie quickly pointed out.

Nothing like being put on the spot is there. "Well I don't know, I don't feel comfortable having you around. You've treated me as if I was a piece of shit and I really don't think that you should be a part of our lives anymore."

"Sarah I...I... I have no respect for you." She yelled coarsely. "You fucked with Jen while you were still with Robbie. She told me that today."

That evil cow was not gonna leave without a bitch fight, I had to state my case fast and put Kiera in her place once and for all.

"You are the most vindictive bastard I have had the displeasure to meet. You cannot force Robbie to fall in love with you when she clearly has no intension in getting into your knickers. And by the way you have a face like a fucking ferret, your eyes are too close together and I have Robbie and you don't." Oh how I've missed being a sarcastic bitch.

Her face reddened with anger and she had no come back for those sentimental remarks she had so delightfully just received. Her exit was pretty grand as she walked out of the door with her head held high she turned around and said. "Well at least I stay true to my partners; slut."

Her leaving was the best thing ever, Charlie high fived me and Jessica had to run for a pee as she had been desperate to go but didn't want to miss out on any of the fun.

"I'm sorry Robbie; I just lowered myself down to her level didn't I. And I'm sorry about what went on with Jen. It meant nothing and technically we had broken up." I had never felt as disgusted with myself as I did right at this very moment for allowing myself to have fallen for Jens evil ways.

"Sarah, Sarah, its ok I thought we had moved on from that." She assured me yet again.

"I know, but I just feel so fucking guilty over it." I snuggled in to Robbie's shoulder and she stroked my hair attentively.

"This isn't going to change a thing between us. I love you Sarah, please trust my judgement." She had become my new hero and protector of my vanity.

Kate made an arrh noise and Charlie recommended that we make a toast. "Let's make a toast to new beginnings; plenty of great sex and some crazy love connections." We all cheered and drank to that.

CHAPTER SEVENTEEN

HOW SHE MET MY MOTHER

*A*rriving back at the apartment we found the front door had been left wide open and the entire place had been trashed. The worst room hit was our bedroom. The bed linens were slashed and the curtains ripped from the pole. All of my clothes had been flung around and spray painted. We didn't need to guess too hard to which culprit could have done this.

"Should I call the police?" Robbie asked as she began to search to see if anything was missing.

"No, no, we both know what's happened here as long as I never have to see her again. I will smack her so hard if she ever comes near me." I began to pick up the remnants to see if anything could be saved but she had taken great care to make sure that they couldn't.

Knowing that crazy bitch had ruined most of my stuff we binned it all and decided that the apartment needed to be fixed up anyway. So over the next few days I refilled my closet with some amazing bargains and we bought new soft furnishings that complimented who we were as a couple. They also belonged to us and not just me this time.

Kiera had totally disappeared from our lives god only knows where she had vanished to and to be honest who even cared. Jessica was settling in nicely at Kate's and Charlie just doted on her. The change in her attitude towards this relationship was amazing, she was actually being monogamous. My bond with Robbie was growing stronger and it felt like the rest of the world didn't exist when I was with her.

Just after having a major sex session we lay naked on the sofa complimenting each other on our salacious performances when there was the sound of a key turning in the door. "Only me darling, Sarah; are you home?"

Chapter Seventeen: How She Met My Mother

"Shit! Shit, it's my mother, quick run." We both shot up from our frolicking antics grabbing pillows to cover up our exposed parts and made it to the bedroom just in the nick of time.

"Hi mum, I'll be out in a minute, we're just getting dressed." I yanked some clothes off the hangers and frantically tried to put something on before she had time to guess what we had just been up to.

"Are you in the bedroom Sarah?" I could hear her making her way towards our door as she called out.

"Yes mum, just give us a minute." My efforts to get dressed under such pressure were proving to be quite difficult as Robbie kept fooling around delaying my attempts.

"So that's your mother." She giggled as she took a sneak peek through the door.

"Yes it is and what a fucking way for her to meet you." I whispered trying to zip up my jeans.

"Sarah I'll put the kettle on shall I." Mum called from the kitchen.

"Ok mum, you know where everything is. C'mon Robbie hurry, I'm not going out there by myself." I tied my hair back tightly to make it appear neater and shoved the empty hangers back into the closet slamming the doors shut behind me to hide the clutter.

"Oh honey relax, she must know her little girl gets up to a bit of the old slap and tickle from time to time. Oh my god I wonder if she can smell the sex?" She playfully tugged at my clothing pulling me around but I wasn't responding to it.

We finally emerged from the bedroom fully dressed and looking a little flustered. I kissed my mother on her cheek and then grabbed some cups out of the cupboard behind her.

"Who's your friend Sarah and does she want milk in her tea?" She stood there holding the carton ready for action.

"Oh mum this is Robbie, Robbie this is my mother." This was going to be interesting.

"Hi Mrs Niles it's so nice to meet you at last. I've heard so many delightful stories about you." That was polite I thought.

"You're Robbie, the one Sarah married? You're the one who left her with a broken heart and in a right state." That wasn't so polite.

"Mum please I don't want you to talk to Robbie like that. It's not like that; I caused most of that mess and I deserved what I got." No bloody way was I going to tell her what I did though.

"Well if you ask me, you girls should be more aware of your feelings towards each other and stop playing these hurtful games. So Robbie do you think you're here to stay this time?" Ouch! She really was on the defensive side today and I wasn't too sure where she was going with this.

"Mrs Niles I love your daughter very much, and yes I know we had a rocky start and we'll probably come across more bumps in the future, but I think that our relationship is in a strong place now and I'm not about to give up on that." She placed her hand over the top of mine giving me the reassurance that everything was still cool between us.

"Well I'm glad to hear that Robbie dear. I needed to know that my daughter is in safe hands. The last time I checked she was with her friend Charlie, nice girl that one." She passed the drinks around and opened up a packet of biscuits placing them in a formal pattern on the plate.

"Oh Charlie's with Jessica now!" I stupidly blurted out without thinking.

My mother spilt her tea down her front in hearing the shocking news that my pregnant friend had landed herself a good woman to sleep with.

"Oh we're all still good mates mum, and Jessica has now moved in with Kate." Let's just confuse the old dear even further shall we.

"Who on earth is Kate? And I thought you said she was with Charlie." She took a tea towel out of the top drawer next to the sink and patted her blouse with it in an attempt to dry the stain.

"She's Robbie's ex and now best friend and has very kindly rented half of her house out to Jessica, making it possible for her and the baby to have a real home." I couldn't help think that to the outsider this must all sound like total bullshit.

Chapter Seventeen: How She Met My Mother

"She's having a baby, I don't understand, I thought two women couldn't." Oh my poor confused mummy.

"No mum its Jake's. And Jessica is getting a restraining order against him because... oh never mind mum there's just too much info to go through right now." I could see the look of confusion on her face as I hadn't filled her in on any of the latest gossip; something in which she had become accustomed to.

"So is Jake still on the scene or has he moved on?" Her eyes were wide as she listened intently to the information being passed around. She was enjoying becoming a little gossip queen on the side.

"Oh he's with the lovely Jen now." Robbie willingly piped up.

"Yes mum, he wants to be in the baby's life he's made that perfectly clear but I think he has to get over himself first." I nudged Robbie's foot with mine to let her know that too much info was being passed on and we needed to change the subject.

"Well every child needs a father in its life; just look how well my Sarah turned out." Oh if only she knew half the shit that I'd got up to she'd think twice about that comment.

"So mum what brings you here today anyway?" I'd forgotten that she had turned up unexpectedly.

"Well your father has gone to look at a vintage car that he's interested in buying, so I thought I'd wait here until he's done." She never was very patient when it came to my father and his hobbies.

"Well then Mrs Niles would you like some more biscuits to go with your tea?" Robbie offered the rest of the plate to her and she took three with no intention on devouring them.

"Please dear call me Judy; after all you are family now. So I suppose I might as well say what's on my mind and get it out in the open: You're never going to make me a grandmother then." She was digging deep with the sharp remarks and I wasn't sure if it was a case of protecting her one and only daughter's reputation or if indeed she actually was resentful of the fact that I had opted out of the baby producing market.

"Mother that's enough; I've never said that I wanted children anyhow." The small talk wasn't working and I was quite disappointed with her comments. My goal was to get everyone to gel together harmoniously and it was proving to be a rather tricky task.

"Sarah darling I have no idea what to think or expect from you these days, and if I don't ask how am I ever going to know anything." She was clearly getting flustered and I could see that she was just going to keep rambling on about my personal life until she heard the answers only she wanted to hear.

"Ok mum, obviously we're not going to bare you any grandchildren that's a guarantee, and to be honest things are good just the way they are. We don't need to add any more complications to our lives." With having Jen and then Kiera trying to plant their claws into our relationship I think I had made a fairly grown up decision, but it was something that I had to discuss with Robbie at a later date as I had no idea how she felt on the subject and I had made assumptions about our future together without consulting her first.

There was a knock on the door; it was my father, his face was beaming with a relatively wide smile due to the fact that he had fallen in love with the car that he had just visited and the offer he made on it had been accepted.

"Hi angel how's it going?" Not bloody well that's for sure.

"Hi daddy this is Robbie, the one I told you about at Christmas." Always the gentleman he nodded his head and politely shook her hand and welcomed her to the family in his usually reserved manner. He was a reliable type of chap and I knew that I could count on his discretion not to make me feel as though I was a failure in his eyes for choosing the path that I was on, which just so happens to be the one that I want to be on.

Conversation was kept to a light pleasant order for half an hour before my parents decided that it was time to make their way back home. I was quite relieved when they left and knowing the way that my mother works she was probably dominating the topic all the way home with baby talk without giving a thought to my father's exciting news about his new baby.

"Oh my god Robbie I'm so sorry, totally, totally embarrassing." If there was a boot camp for training parents to behave themselves I would be the first to send mine there.

"No it wasn't, I didn't mind them at all. I actually think your parents are pretty cool people."

Maybe Robbie hadn't been introduced to too many of her ex girlfriends parents in the past so she didn't have much to compare mine with.

"Really; so you don't think they're a little on the strange side? I do." I checked myself out in the mirror for clarification that I wasn't about to turn into my mother in the near future; nope still looking pretty chic right now.

"Well I see where you get your personality from if that's what you mean." She joked amused at my quest to lead a normal dignified life.

"Oi you bloody cheeky mare." I gave her a light pinch on her bum in a playful way which turned into a game of tickle each other in the ribs. Our moods were on a joyful high as we teased and entertained ourselves which just happened to take us to our next activity; pleasurable sex games; my favourite.

Later that day we decided to go and visit Kate and Jessica to see how they were getting on with their new living arrangement. Upon arriving and expecting a calm serene union we were greeted with lots of screaming that seemed to be coming from the lounge. We both ran in to the house not knowing what to expect. Jessica was standing by the window and completely flipping out at Jake, with Jen at his side looking slutty and extremely evocative. Jessica was exhausted and distressed even though she was the one doing most of the shouting.

I quickly marched over to my friend's side and yelled out above the noise of everyone's overactive voices. "What the hell is going on?"

"Oh Sarah they just won't leave me alone this twat seems to think that he can take the baby away from me when it's born." The pitch of her voice was high and she spoke too fast for me to catch everything she was saying, then she began to hyperventilate so I sat her down and fanned her with a magazine that Robbie grabbed from the table behind her.

"What the hell Jake, where do you get off harassing a pregnant woman like this." If only I was a guy I would have knocked him out by now.

"Shut the fuck up Sarah this has nothing to do with you." He snarled like a rabid dog.

"Oh you think so, it has everything to do with me you ass, she's my friend and what makes you think that you can take the baby away? You had better get yourself a damn good lawyer matey boy." I was adamant on standing my ground with this jerk, all he had achieved by this ridiculous behaviour was the confirmation that Jessica would definitely need to distance herself from him.

"It's my baby too and I don't feel she's going to make a fit mother. Just look at her shacking up with another woman, it's not natural. She's not normal!" I couldn't believe what a fucking hypocrite he was being. After all he was the one who had exploited and introduced her into this lifestyle.

Jen had remained quiet through all of this which struck me as unusual but I knew that she was the main instigator of it all. Their act of poor manners had become tiresome and boring and it was time for them to take their performance to a different venue; like maybe on a cruise ship where they could both mysteriously fall overboard and be eaten by sharks. No such luck! My instincts led me to the door where I opened it wide, took a deep breath and gave a few thoughts of my own.

"You're a fucking wanker Jake, now you and your tart can leave. I can't believe you've put Jessica through this. The stress can do a great deal of harm to the baby; now both of you get out." How on earth could he define his life as normal with that crazy cow still hanging on his arm?

As they left Jen hissed out at Jessica. "This isn't over bitch!" Her eyes had become wide and full of hate and I dreaded to think what sort of plan she was going to concoct next.

Chapter Seventeen: How She Met My Mother

I slammed the door hard behind them and headed straight over to the drink cabinet and poured myself a brandy: Something I'd never drank before but it seemed like the right thing to do at the time and I hated the burning sensation it gave as I swigged it down in one high speed gulp but at least it stopped me from shaking with anger. Once the hot reaction had finished stripping the top layer of skin from the inside of my mouth I offered everyone else a drink as I poured myself a second glass, Robbie took me up on the offer as she was a little stunned and shaken up herself. Then Jessica broke down into tears and kept repeating in a broken scared voice. "What am I going to do? What am I going to do?" She tried to get up quickly but collapsed back into the chair and sobbed loudly. I knelt down beside her and promised that we would all do what we could to protect her and the baby.

"First of all you have to see your solicitor and get a restraining order for both of them. You have witnesses to his behaviour and I bet my last fucking pay check that this is all down to Jen."

Her eyes were swollen and red from all the crying and I gently wiped the tears away from her cheeks and stroked her hair just like my mother would do to me when things had gotten the better of me. I noticed that the strain of this pregnancy had begun to take a spiteful twist to her looks. The usual stunning beauty that used to be my reflective image had changed into a tired saddened wreck. She deserved better than this.

"I'm sorry that I didn't listen to you Sarah, I was blinded by the wall of lies she fed me, and he's just as bad. If I hadn't got pregnant none of this would be happening right now." My friend was hurting and she needed me more than ever now.

"My sweet innocent Jessica, you have been blessed with the chance to reproduce life; this is the most remarkable achievement anyone can reach." I whispered to her whilst stroking her hand reassuringly. "It will all turn out fine in the end; you just have a few hurdles to get over first."

I looked up at Robbie; our smiles were linked with softness, and in one tender moment affectionate warmth melted my heart. I knew just how precious she was to me and how close I had got to losing her for good. Why is there so much drama in lesbian land I thought?

Kate was a little disturbed by all of the commotion and opted to go to bed as it wasn't in her nature to get involved in aggressive behaviour. We finally managed to calm Jessica down and encouraged her to get some well deserved rest.

Robbie stood in front of me and lovingly caressed my neck as she pulled me in closer to her. Leaning in towards me she softly kissed my lips with a heartfelt nature that sent tingles running down my spine and made my heart beat faster with each intake of breath.

"I love you so much Sarah." She whispered delicately.

My eyes welled up and a single tear rolled down my cheek as a surge of intense emotions rushed through my body. The knowledge that my entire life was revolving around another's was a very welcomed wake up call, I now felt complete.

"Please don't ever let us get to the same spite that Jessica and Jake have between them. Promise me Robbie, if it doesn't work out between us that we'll be more adult about it."

"Hey shush pretty girl, I think we're solid enough and no more talk about breaking up, my world has been rocked by you." We hugged each other squeezing tightly making sure that neither one of us had any intensions of going anywhere else.

We were shortly interrupted by Kate calling us from upstairs. She had heard a disturbance going on outside and realised that Jen and Jake were still around. "I think there's an extra episode of the Jen and Jake saga going on. Can you make sure that all the doors are locked please I don't trust them."

"Ok Kate I'm on it now." Robbie called back; releasing me from her hold.

We ran to the window to witness the showdown on display. Jessica; without delay joined us and listened in to what they had to say. I told her to close the window as she really didn't need to hear what they were bitching about her. Then she stuck her head out of the opening and concentrated on the voices screaming louder as Jen was becoming hysterically melodramatic and creating an embarrassing scene for all the neighbours to watch.

"You're not a man at all Jake." She squealed right in his face. "You make me sick; you should have stayed with that bitch of a wife instead of wasting my time."

"Just listen to me Jen." He pleaded like an ass and had to grab both of her wrists to stop her from physically attacking him. "I only married her so I could further my career. She could have been anyone; I didn't actually want her she's fucking useless to me but the stupid cow was in love with me so I manipulated her into marriage. It's just that having a baby wasn't in my plans."

"Well the shits hit the fan for you then." She spat out furiously. "I don't want you Jake, I was only in this so that I could destroy Sarah's world; she interfered with mine, the fucking hoar. And she was a lousy fuck, I hope you can hear me bitch!" She screamed up to the house still struggling to free her wrists from Jakes power of control then stopped momentarily and stared up at the window waiting for a reply, but she didn't get one.

"Oh just fuck off Jake, you useless piece of shit." She shrieked and then after managing to break free from her captor got into a black BMW and sped off down the street with tires screeching and narrowly missing an oncoming car. Jake was left abandoned in the middle of the street to make his own way back to his hell hole.

Robbie closed the window and guided Jessica back to the comfort of the armchair and compassionately reassured her that she was better off not hearing anymore of the negative comments that were being thrown her way. But her tears began to flow again causing her cheeks to turn a deep red and her nose to sniffle profusely. This poor lost soul had been deceived so cruelly by what she thought was someone who she could trust; Jen had been completely dilettante and used her subjects to their fullest capacity in her game of seek and vengeance.

"He never wanted me." she cried. "He just used me. I really loved him in the beginning Sarah and I thought he loved me but he changed his behaviour as soon as he met Jen. He's a complete fake, the way he flirted with me when he was still seeing you and how he looked into my eyes, I feel so humiliated."

I could see she was searching for answers but what could I say. Hey he was ok for a fuck when I was pissed out of my tree. I didn't like the guy ever, and I had only used him in the same way that he had done to my friend.

"Sweetheart the hurt will go away, I know because I've been there: remember. You have to hit rock bottom to be able to get better again. And it will get better. You have Charlie now and I know she loves you." Her glazed eyes widened and she managed to produce a tiny smile from the corner of her mouth; the mere mention of Charlie's name caused her to lighten her mood.

"I know if this shit hadn't have happened I wouldn't have met her, well not in that way I mean. She keeps me sane and I feel very relaxed and safe with her. I think I've fallen in love with her." I was glad that she had found someone that she was able to trust and confide in as well as me.

"Well that's a good start, she is an amazing person and the two of you are pretty cute together. Now you need to focus on this relationship and move forward. Robbie do you think Kate would mind if we stayed the night?" My friend was going to have all the security she needed tonight just let them bloody well try anything else.

"I'm sure she'll be fine with that. We can camp out in the study." Umm cozy.

The next morning we all sat in the garden under the gazebo eating a breakfast of fresh fruit and croissants and making jokes at Jens expense then the jingle on Jessica's phone began to play and when she looked at it she said Jake had just left her a text message. She stared at it for a while in anticipation that she was in for another round of drama.

"So are you going to read it?" I asked, eagerly trying to pry into her affairs.

"Ok hold on, he says that Jen broke up with him last night and that he's sorry for making my life hell lately and that it was Jen being vindictive towards you and Robbie. Oh my god, he wants to step aside and let me raise the baby, I can have sole custody Sarah." Her chin began to quiver as she held her tears back but I couldn't help thinking what a cop out. He was abandoning his responsibilities as a father figure, the least thing he could do was be supportive and he wasn't even offering her that.

I gave her a kiss on her cheek and a light hug to show my half approval. "That's wonderful; I'm so pleased for you." I told her but it wasn't meant entirely sincere.

"He says he will support us financially and that we can start divorce proceedings immediately. I'm gonna be free of his shit." She clasped her hands together delighted that her day had begun on such a positive note.

I supposed that this was excellent news for her, but I being the pessimist just didn't trust the fact that Jen had turned over a new leaf and found closure with Robbie. Just thinking of the crap she has handed out gives me shudders.

"Do you think Jen will leave us all alone now Robbie?" I knew she was hoping that Jen would completely disappear for convenience sake if nothing else and her experience with Jen's vicious and delicious behaviour had given her knowledgeable insight into a mind so full of delusion.

"Oh Sarah I've had a long journey with taking her abuse, she has a really nasty habit of reappearing when you least expect it. She doesn't go away too easily, so I have no idea if she's gone for good." That sounded like expert advice. But this was a worrying fact and the not knowing was just as bad as if she was on the prowl.

For a short moment we were all in deep thought about how unprepared we were for her next round of tricks if she was to continue when the doorbell rang making us jump. Robbie got up and offered to go and see who it was and we were all relieved to see that it was Charlie making an entrance.

"Hey babe, you ok. Why didn't you call me last night?" Jessica flung her arms around Charlie's neck and held on tightly only relaxing her hold after several minutes of petting and kissing. Once they were all loved up Jessica explained her reasons for not contacting Charlie and all was forgiven.

There was a major discussion mostly based on Jessica's future and how serious Charlie really was about her. The outcome was Charlie and Jessica were going to cohabitate, this was with Kate's approval and we all had to be on our guard no matter what.

CHAPTER EIGHTEEN
DESTINATION LOVE

Within two days Charlie had moved in with help from Jezz and Jules, and I attempted baking a red velvet cake, for love, not that it looked picturesque, the sides were burnt and the frosting was too runny. But it was the offer that counted.

"You don't have to eat it if you don't want to. I know it looks rancid, but it was my first attempt at baking." I prayed it tasted better than it looked.

Charlie cut a rather large slice and made a yummy face. "It's good Sarah; it doesn't have to look good to taste good, right Jessica." She gave Jessica a sly wink thinking that I hadn't caught it.

"Oh right Charlie." She replied taking a small bite. I knew they were just humouring me, it was bloody awful; after taking one bite I felt as tho I had just eaten the remnants of a car seat belt.

Charlie asked me how come Jessica never lived with me and I laughed out loud when she asked this. I informed her that we shared my place when we first moved to London but the problem was that we were, and still are too much alike. We both left the housework for the midnight fairies to do, we'd turn up with a guest or two at all hours of the day or night without a care for each other's privacy and occupying the bathroom was a nightmare; it was never vacant long enough for the other housemate to enjoy using. No I think our friendship means much more to us just the way it is.

But on a more serious note paranoia had set in with us all and Robbie made sure I got to work safely by escorting me back and forth, her eyes were constantly darting everywhere checking each street that we crossed, and a feeling of unrest and long pauses in between each conversation took place. Whilst working at the store I would look up at every customer that walked through the doorway making sure they weren't Jen. These actions were driving me nuts.

It was several days later when we all let our guards finally take a break. I had felt resentful to the fact that a mere idea of a person had taken complete control of our lives.

It was Friday morning and I had just opened up the store when my parents paid me a surprise visit.

"Mum! Dad! What are you doing here; I mean what a nice surprise."

"Sarah darling we thought we'd um..."

"What your mother is trying to say, if you don't mind me interrupting you Judy, is that we only have one daughter and we like to visit her every now and then." He was right of course.

"Sorry daddy, I didn't mean to be rude." I had to stop acting so jumpy and relax a little.

"So how are things with you and Robbie?" My mother asked picking up a small jumper from the display stand and inspecting it in a rather peculiar manner. I couldn't imagine her purchasing such an item as it wasn't even big enough to cover up one tit but the young girls seemed to favour its style.

"Oh great, we're so in love, she's just great, everything is great. So what do you think of my new store I'm intrigued to know what you think of it." How many times can I say great without it sounding like it's not so great with the threat of Jen still hanging over us?

"It's lovely dear. I see you have lots of customers browsing you must be doing well for yourself and we're very proud of you. But I don't understand what that girl is doing over there." My father pointed over to a corner and nodded.

"What girl? I can't see." As I looked over his shoulder I could see a woman dressed in a long leather coat, her hair tied back tightly and a large pair of dark sunglasses sitting on her face. She was placing flyers in between all the merchandise. As I approached her I realised that it was Jen and she seemed pretty happy with herself. I knew whatever she was up to wasn't going to be good. My heart was racing fast as she had gained my complete attention and distracted me from spending time with my parents.

Chapter Eighteen: Destination Love

"What the hell are you doing here? Get out before I call the police." I shoved her away from the corner and escorted her toward the door keeping a tight grip on her arm.

"Everyone's gonna know about you Sarah. You don't deserve Robbie, you have no passion. You're not a true lesbian you're just in it for the thrill." She shoved me back and made her way over to the center of the store and carried on handing her leaflets out. I picked one up that she had placed down and couldn't believe what I was reading.

Attention everyone the woman serving you in this store is Sarah Niles. She thinks she is a lesbian! She likes to get so drunk so she can take it up the ass. She will shag anyone who wants her. Her marriage is fraudulent. She married another woman just to keep her in the country. For a good time call... And there was my number written in big bold letters at the bottom of the page. This bitch's timing was impeccable.

"Sarah darling what is this about?" My mother quizzed holding one of the flyers in her hand, my father leant over her shoulder to read it and I could see it slowly being absorbed into his brain. He removed the note from my mother's hand and crumpled it up before throwing it into the bin.

"Look here young lady." He said directly to Jen and walked right up to her and stared her directly in the eye. "I don't know what your game is but I think you are a pretty sick woman and you need some professional help."

He started to pick up the notes she had so nicely spread around but Jen was having none of it. I was her target and she wasn't finished with me yet. She raised her voice and made sure that everyone could hear. "This bitch likes me to tie her up and beat her across her ass with my leather strap. She also likes to be fucked by strangers and she's a cheater." She was breathing heavy and her words were spoken in great anger as she broadcast my private life to all my customers and my parents.

My father had just about had enough of her foulness and trying to humiliate me in public. He announced to the customers that the store was closed and to please vacate immediately. This included my mother. And as the last person left he locked the glass door and turned around slowly in the direction of Jen to confront her.

"What is it that you want from my daughter?" He walked right over to her and his height towered hers and I thought for one second that he was going to pound her.

"Your daughter well isn't this fucking cozy. First of all she can do us all a favour and die." Her eyes were red and swollen and her jaw was clenched as she showed such anger and hatred toward me. I genuinely believed that she wanted me dead. My father carried on speaking to her calmly trying to keep the situation under control.

"Look young lady I don't know what your problem is but I'm sure this can all be sorted out amicably." He pulled his cheque book out from his jacket pocket ready to pay her off and be rid of her.

"Sorted; do you not have any idea what your daughter has been up to? She has destroyed my life; she doesn't deserve to be happy, she's not good enough for Robbie, she's just another piece of trash I have to deal with."

"Jen I have no idea why you think that Robbie would want you after everything you have put her through." This was one hell of a crazy bitch but probably not a good time to tell her that right now.

"She would have come back to me if you hadn't got in my way. I need you out of the equation you slut." She undid the zip on her coat and revealed a pushed up cleavage from a tight bra and a short leather skirt that just covered her knickers. Her sex appeal was extremely intense and controlling and I was sure that she had intended to intimidate me with her sexual attraction but it wasn't working.

"Now wait a moment Jen, is that your name Jen? My daughter deserves happiness just like we all do, so screaming out obscenities in public isn't going to help the situation is it." Go team dad.

"Oh shut up, what do you know? This little cow shags anything that moves. You raised a slut you idiot." Not a good word to call my father; attended university has a bachelor's degree you know what I'm saying here.

Chapter Eighteen: Destination Love

"Hey leave my father alone Jen, you don't need to do this. Please leave us all in peace for god sake." Her mental disorder was growing tiresome with me and I was quietly relieved when I heard knocking on the door and saw Robbie waiting anxiously to get in. My protector was here to save my honour so I ran over to release the lock and gave her a fast explanation of what was going on.

"Oh look who's here; now you're showing interest." Jen snarled as her mood intensified.

"You have to stop this harassment Jen; I have absolutely nothing to offer you. What we had was sick and disturbing. I had personal problems and you jumped in on my weakness and used it. It was a dark time in my life and I really want to forget about it. I don't want you!" She shouldn't have to be explaining this in front of my father, hell I didn't even know most of this stuff.

"You fucking bitch, you used me and then threw me away like trash when something better came along." A piece of her long hair stuck to her deep red lipstick and she tried to act as though it wasn't irritating her but I could see that it clearly was.

"It wasn't like that Jen. I wasn't thinking straight back then. I think you wanted more than I could give you." She was pleading with this woman but nothing was getting through to her.

"No, no I didn't. You felt something for me I know you did. You gave me your soul." What would this cow know about souls?

"My soul was empty Jen. I needed you to hurt me, I needed to feel pain. I told you I didn't care what you did to me. I'm sorry if you got the impression that you thought I was yours. You've wasted all this time waiting for me, for nothing." Maybe she should calm down on the honesty just for now I was beginning to feel that my father was being forced to listen to too much trashy information.

"I hate you Robbie and I hate that slut you married. Maybe immigration services should be informed about this farce." What a snitch!

"I must say that my daughter is genuinely in love with Robbie." My father put his arm around me showing his support for my relationship with my wife and I was proud to be standing at his side.

"Oh shut up granddad." She was pushing her luck insulting my dad like that. He doesn't have any grandchildren yet. But I really wanted to knock her block off. Hearing her talk to my father like that was quite disturbing.

"You dykes are all the same you'll get what you deserve, you just wait." With those remarks she grabbed a large pile of jeans that I had so neatly stacked and tossed them across the floor before storming out and ranting that she wasn't finished with me.

"Are you ok did she hurt you?" Robbie asked as she hugged me tightly.

"Yes I'm fine thanks." Just a bruised ego and a few embarrassing moments in front of my father that's all.

"Mr Niles I'm so sorry that you had to hear all of that." I think that Robbie was slightly embarrassed too.

"Please Robbie call me dad. I do consider you to be my daughter now. I may not say too much most of the time, but my heart is in the right place." Isn't he sweet?

"Thanks Mr N. I mean dad." She gave him a quick hug and then returned back to my open arms squeezing me tighter than she had ever done before.

"Now I'm going to get your mother she must be worried. I suggest you two get this place back in order so you can let all of those high spending customers back in." He never was one to let things affect him too much.

"Thanks dad I love you." I felt a little emotional saying that as I hadn't said it enough in the past.

"I love you too Sarah, now take care of this place and I'll see you later." And off he went to rescue my mother from her own worrying thoughts.

We tidied up and put things back in their rightful place and opened back up for business. Robbie spent the rest of the day with me, helping out and chatting to customers and making some pretty decent sales for me. I felt proud to watch her in action. We also phoned Kate to let everyone know what had happened so they could be prepared

Chapter Eighteen: Destination Love

for any action that cow might to throw at them. During the phone call I could hear people giggling in the background and Kate kept making a shush noise and whispering they'll hear you. I didn't pay too much attention to it as other things had prioritised my mind.

Jessica joined in on the conversation and asked what we had planned for Saturday as she wanted us to come over about 1.30. Again I thought nothing of it as it was not an unusual request and an image of sitting in the garden enjoying a nice lunch and a few glasses of wine crossed my mind.

After making a financial killing in the afternoon we closed up the store and picked up a takeaway on the way home. Of course I had to have my favourite lemon chicken.

It was nice to have a peaceful evening after the events that had occurred earlier. My parents had invited themselves to stay over for the weekend and my mother kept relaying the scare we had all experienced. She was quite annoyed on how rudely Jen had presented herself. Perhaps she'd favour her as an angel if she had an insight to my recent activities, but as far as she was concerned they'd be kept under lock and key and with Robbie reassuring me that it was possible that Jen was out of the picture for good as she had never acted like this before was good news to my ears.

Saturday was upon us and the sun was shining right through the lounge window sending beams of light across the room. Robbie opened the balcony door allowing a fresh breeze to cool us down. I turned on the CD player and a romantic song was playing. She summoned me to her and we danced slowly hugging tightly oblivious that my parents were standing in the room watching us.

"Oh Sarah darling you two look so beautiful together." My mother cried out and clasped her hands together; she had a sweet approving smile on her face.

"Mum, we were just, you know. Anyway you two look nice are you going somewhere special?" Dad was handsomely dressed in a brand new suit and mum was holding a pink hat that matched her pink dress and pink shoes.

"Um yes we are dear and we'll tell you all about it later. Will you be going to see Jessica today at all?" She asked rather coyly.

"Yes mum this afternoon actually, why?" She never asked me that before.

"Oh just give her our love will you dear. We are very fond of her you know." That was a pretty random comment being as she's never involved herself with Jessica's affairs in the past.

"Ok mum will do." Note to one's self don't turn out to be like my mother.

"Well all being well we'll see you both later then. Bye dear, bye Robbie." And off they went on their merry way to do whatever it is that the older generation do.

"So Robbie do you think my parents were acting a little strange? Come to think of it you're acting a little different today as well. Am I missing something here?" I was growing suspicious that something was going on behind my back.

"Can't a girl just show her wife some romantic affection? After all we do have the place to ourselves for a few hours so how about a bit of fooling around?" She took me by the hand and led me into the bedroom where a bottle of champagne rested on a bed of ice in a bucket on the side table and red rose petals had been placed all over the floor.

"Robbie what's going on?" This was a beautiful gesture and I was extremely flattered by the whole ensemble.

"Shush, I'm showing you a token of my love. I do love you Sarah Niles Page. I love everything about you, even your stubbornness, your naivety, your intelligence and your beauty. In a short space of time I have seen you grow from a spoilt brat who needed to be the center of attention into a warm loving person with a big heart. We have something so rare and special between us. Now take off your clothes and lay down over here." She showed me the bed and I respected her wishes.

I undressed slowly, capturing her full attention, and snuggled up next to her on the bed. She picked up an ice cube from the champagne bucket and gradually ran it down the back of my neck, then

Chapter Eighteen: Destination Love

slipped it over my breasts allowing it to melt over my nipples. The sensation from the cold droplets of water encouraged them to stand erect and then she glided her warm tongue over them, sending me into an insane need to be fucked. As she entered me with her fingers she kept her face level with mine, watching my every expression as I felt the enjoyment of her thrusts. I loved her watching me, I was at my most vulnerable as she saw my weakness entwine itself with my strength. My inner soul belonged to her and as she brought me to orgasm she kissed me hard on the lips making me breathless and internally euphoric.

We lay naked fondling each other for an hour when she said. "I have a surprise for you this afternoon."

"You do! What is it? Can I have a clue? Is it large? Is it expensive?" Could I ask any more questions, I was tiring myself out?

"Whoa, slow down, no guessing. All I want you to do is dress in your most elegant outfit. Now that's all I'm telling you. C'mon let's take a shower together and then get ready, Jessica is expecting us shortly." She playfully rolled me over to the edge of the bed where I came face to face with the bottle of bubbly.

"So are we going to open the champagne?" What was she celebrating?

"No not yet that's for later. You'll see." She was being too secretive.

Our shower together was seductive and sensual and I felt a new energy in our relationship as she lovingly cleansed my skin with my oversized pink sponge. After drying I went into the bedroom and searched for something to wear. I chose a long white floaty dress that had shoestring halter neck ties. It was an item I had bought after the Kieragate incident but didn't have an occasion in mind when I purchased it. I piled my hair up high on top of my head allowing a few wispy bits to hang down and only wore a light touch of make up giving me an innocent natural glow.

Looking at my reflection in the mirror I could see the person that Robbie saw in me; here stood the softer kinder Sarah. I made my announcement that I was coming out of the bedroom telling her to close her eyes until I said otherwise.

"Ok you can open them now!" I felt really special and feminine.

"Wow you look like a Greek Goddess. Turn around let me see you. You look perfect Sarah." She was admiring me with such authenticity and I welcomed her approval.

"Thank you kind lady, I do feel elegant, you don't think it's too much do you?" I had no idea if I was overdressed for the surprise occasion.

"Now didn't I just say you look perfect?" She went into the bedroom to change and I was amazed when she reappeared wearing the same white suit that I had first met her in. It really showed off the blueness in her eyes; I just couldn't help but be mesmerised by them.

"Oh Robbie please tell me where we're going I can't stand it." I begged.

"No not yet now the taxi is here so you'll know soon." She picked up the camera and several poses later we were ready to leave.

We arrived at Kate's and as we got out of the taxi we were greeted by a house decorated in white streamers and white and silver balloons. The front door was already open and people's voices were coming from the back garden. We walked through to the back of the house and were greeted by a loud cheer of (Surprise!) A glass of champagne found its way into my hand just as Robbie turned to face me and said. "Marry me Sarah. I mean properly, for love. Will you marry me?"

I knew the journey that we had both recently travelled had been emotionally intense but everything felt so right.

"I love you more than life Robbie, yes, yes I will marry you." I was honoured to be in such wonderful company and for Robbie to want to marry me properly; I couldn't have wished for anything better.

Everyone cheered and toasted to the announcement and I could feel myself trembling with excitement as I looked around to see who all these people were. My parents were standing there with huge smiles on their faces. I should have known they were up to something. Jessica came marching up with a bouquet of flowers and winked at me as she shoved them in my hand and Charlie fixed a carnation on Robbie's lapel.

Kate gave us both a big hug and said that she was glad to be present at this ceremony. I was glad to have her there too. My cheeks were beginning to hurt from the constant smiling but I just couldn't stop.

"Ok gather round everyone." Robbie called out.

We put our drinks down on the table beside us and turned to face each other. Then she held both my hands as she began to make her speech.

"Sarah I know that we have already placed our vows legally, so this is not an official ceremony, but for me it is real. I vow to love you forever, to make you smile every day, I vow to keep you safe and be your protector. I vow to support you in decisions that you make in life. I vow to work hard every day at keeping our relationship fresh and real. I love you Sarah."

"Robbie I have nothing prepared as this was an unexpected surprise a very pleasant one tho. But I will say that, I vow to love you always, to respect your decisions, I vow to learn to cook properly for you, I vow to be your lover as well as your best friend; I vow to give you my heart and my soul. But most of all I vow to be truthful and faithful to you because without you my soul is lost." We sealed the deal with a long heartfelt kiss and I could see that my mother had completely turned into a happy emotional wreck with tears of joy gushing down her cheeks.

"Sarah you look so beautiful sweetheart, I'm sorry we couldn't say anything earlier but Robbie swore us to secrecy." She lifted her hat up slightly to get a better look at me and my image met her approval with great pleasure.

"That's ok mum it was worth it. I'm glad you're both here you soppy pair."

"Um your mother and I want to give you a wedding gift. We bought you a holiday to the South of France and there's a cheque too for some spending money." Wow honeymoon sorted.

"Thanks dad that's a wonderful gift but you didn't have to do that you know." But I'm glad they did. I showed them my gratitude with lots of kisses and waved the cheque teasingly in Robbie's face.

We were presented with lots of gifts and cards and Kate gave us a fabulous gift of equal shares in her business. With having been so ill she wanted someone that she could trust to take it on.

Jessica and Charlie were seated on an old stone bench in front of the lavender bushes and it looked as tho they were having a small celebration of their own.

"Robbie, Sarah, come over here." Charlie called out with laughter in her voice. "We have an announcement of our own to make." We wondered over to them sipping our champagne and holding hands as we were so in love.

"What's up?" I asked as we approached their giggling as if they had a little secret of their own.

"I've just asked Jessica to marry me and she's accepted." Charlie really was smitten and I was so proud of her.

"Oh that's fantastic news you guys." Oh how weddings bring out the best in people.

"We're going to bring the baby up together. By the way it's a girl, we found out yesterday. Jake has also agreed to let Charlie adopt her. She will have full parental rights." Charlie would make a wonderful parent with her patience and calm capabilities.

This was a glorious day all round as so much joy and happiness was in the air. Each and every one of us had been on our own journey in life, maybe in different directions but all reaching the same destination: Destination love.

THE END